The Messenger

Rudy Cain

Lacey Deaver

Published by
World Video Bible School®
25 Lantana Lane
Maxwell, Texas 78656
www.wvbs.org

Copyright 2016 World Video Bible School®
Story Copyright 2016 Rudy Cain

All rights reserved. No part of this book may be reproduced or copied in any form without permission from WVBS.
Printed in the USA.

ISBN: 978-0-9967003-4-4

Cover art by Aubrie Deaver

Layout by Aubrie Deaver

Cover photo from freeimages.com

All Scripture quotations are from The New King James Version of the Bible, unless otherwise specified. Copyright 1982, Thomas Nelson, Inc.

Serving the Church since 1986

wvbs.org

The Story:

This fictional story was given to
me by my grandfather, Rudy Cain.

May God receive the glory.

Special thanks to:

Aubrie Deaver and her work in transcribing
the story from oral words to printed page.

**Special thanks to those
who proofed this book:**

Elizabeth Beall
Loretta Horner
Sharon Cain
Rachel Howard
Patty Shafer

To the lives of my loved ones who have already gone on ahead.
I'll see you soon.

Lacey Deaver

"And as it is appointed for men to die once, but after this the judgment," - Hebrews 9:27

I walked down the maze of sterile hallways, trying to block everything out of my mind. The result was serene indifference to what was happening around me. The only time I paused to re-enter reality was when I reached the revolving door of the hospital. I stepped out into the cool September breeze and stopped just over the threshold.

For months, I had been carefully building a wall around the thoughts that now threatened to break open and pull my entire stream of consciousness into a black hole of fear. I pulled up my jacket collar and felt my hands shaking against the fabric. Closing my eyes, I tilted my head back to face the sky.

Father, please give me strength to overcome my fears. I know the only thing that matters in this life is You. Help me to focus on how I can help others instead of worrying about myself. Show me opportunities to encourage others and point them to You in the time I have left. In Your Son's name, amen.

I felt a peace settling on my heart as those few words drifted through my mind. As my resolve reaffirmed itself and my confidence was restored, I took a deep breath and relaxed my shoulders, opening my eyes to drink in the vista before me. I took in every small detail, appreciating the scenery that only Oregon could boast, as if I had never seen it before, or would again. I admired the golden, red, and nut-brown warmth of the leaves on the trees outside. The wind picked up again, making the leaves dance, some of them parting from the parent stem to be carried off in the autumn air. I smiled. Fall had always been my favorite season.

It was Vicki's favorite, too.

The hospital was built on a rise, surrounded by Douglas Fir trees overlooking the city of Portland. Big trees swayed in the wind on one side, with Portland on the other. Portland boasted grand buildings and majestic bridges spanning the Willamette River that cut through the city, joining the Columbia River, which went on to the Pacific Ocean. She was a beautiful city, the kind best appreciated from a high vantage point. The city where I was born and where I had spent much of my life. My city.

The mid-September crispness in the air cooled my lungs as I breathed it in, along with whispers of memories from my youth of driving through the streets with the top down, the wind tousling my then much darker hair, and the radio going full blast. Today was overcast, yet clear. I could look over and make out the white-capped peak of Mount Saint Helens to the north, then across the city where snowy Mount Hood stood like a magnificent sentry over Portland. Again, fond memories crept through my thoughts of a young boy and his family taking ski trips down that very mountain. I cringed slightly as I recalled that same boy breaking his wrist in a skiing accident down those slopes one Christmas. I looked down and twisted my right hand gently to both sides. The bones had never felt quite the same.

I marveled at the beauty of God's creation: the proud trees and great mountains on one side and in man's creation of the sprawling lights and sounds below. I marveled at how many people went about their existence day to day and were blind to this world so full of wonders, even to the little things which were really blessings for them to contemplate and give them a deeper appreciation for everything they're given in life.

I could almost hear Vicki's voice in my head. *Mal, you're having another soul-thought, aren't you? I can tell. You get that look on your face and then I know you're gone. How about you share it with me?*

I could see her smile, so bright and loving. I felt a gentle kiss on my hand as a rose-colored leaf flitted past in the wind, and I imagined her just behind me, reaching out, waiting for me to turn around.

"Oh, Vicki," I sighed, rubbing the gray hair above my forehead. "How I miss you, my dearest friend."

My watch started to beep in a half-hearted, haphazard way, reminding me both of the time and that my battery was running down. How ironic, I thought to myself as I turned regretfully away from the view of the city.

I checked the time and saw it was 11:30.

"Oh, I need to call her!"

Letting this appointment take complete control of my mind so nothing else could disturb me, I headed out into the parking lot. A cool mist was rising, even this late in the morning, as I opened the glistening door of my red convertible. I rolled down the window, letting the wind continue to wash over me as I sat down and relaxed against the familiar leather seat. It was the kind of car that young men's dreams are made of. I pulled on my seat belt and took out my phone as I drove down the hillside toward the river.

"Hey, how's my beautiful girl today?" I asked when the line picked up and a cheery voice answered. "How about you and I have lunch together this afternoon?"

"Hey, that sounds great!" the young female voice responded gaily. "I wasn't sure you'd be in town today! I'm at the house right now getting some work done, but I could eat anytime!"

"Well, it sounds like a plan," I said with a smile. Just hearing that sweet voice brightened my day more than just about anything else.

The neighborhood of my son's house curved along a winding road which ran up along the more rural side of town after crossing the river. The house I parked in front of was beautiful, designed to look like a modern cabin with a rustic air. A huge brick chimney towered at one end, and a wooden porch wrapped around three quarters of the house. The walls were stone, but the gables had wooden beams that crossed in the center. I stepped out of my car and simply stood gazing fondly at the house, listening to the soft swish of the great fir trees rising skyward behind it. Memories came back of sitting on that very porch watching grandkids chase each other around the yard, relaxing under the eaves on warm summer nights, and long conversations with family members in the dusk of a spring evening. Many a happy hour had passed for me in this place.

Another sight captured my attention as I looked at the house: that of a girl sitting on a deck chair out on the front porch. A curtain of long, strawberry-blond hair cascaded over her shoulders as she bent over the iPad on her lap with her legs tucked up on the chair under her. Her head was lowered so I couldn't see her face, but I could see her forehead puckered in concentration. I had always loved that studious expression on her.

"I hope it's me you're waiting for and not some boy," I called out to her with a twinkle in my eye. She looked up with delight spread over her face when she saw me. Ever since she was a tiny little thing, she had one of the most joyful personalities of anyone I'd ever known.

"Grandpa, you're here!" she exclaimed, bounding up and racing down the porch steps to meet me. Her long hair bounced along behind her and then floated around the two of us as she flew into my arms.

"Hey, kiddo! It's so good to see your face." I hugged her tightly, and she didn't let go of me until I released her long enough to step back and look at her. It did my old heart good. She was my treasure. My pride and joy. I loved her with all my heart. A bittersweet pang pierced me as I realized she was no longer the little girl I still pictured when looking at her. She was a young woman, lovely and beloved.

"It's good to see you, too!" She stepped back and tucked her hair behind her ears, rather unnecessarily since the wind was still blowing pretty strong. Her smile lit up her round, beautiful face with the delicate porcelain skin. "I didn't expect you to call; I thought you might be out of town. Mom and Dad went to Seattle on business today, but they'll be back tomorrow when I leave for school."

"Well, that's alright. It's really you I came to see," I told her, and she glowed.

"Anyway, lunch sounds great to me! I'm starving, and totally up for a break!" she said.

"Oh, well now, I hate to take you away from your studies," I teased her, and chuckled at the sudden grimace on her sweet face.

"Trust me, Grandpa, college Calculus is something I can always find time to get away from for awhile!" she assured me firmly, rolling her green eyes with dramatic flair. I put my arm around her shoulders and kissed the top of her head.

"You do Calculus on your iPad? Wow, the technology these days..."

"Well, I don't think it'd make any difference if I did math on paper or the computer. I still don't think I'll walk away from this class with anything higher than a B."

"You put too much pressure on yourself," I told her. "You're very smart. Give yourself time to embrace the learning curve. I know you'll figure it out and do well, honey."

She shrugged, but smiled. "Thanks, but I'd rather take English Lit again. That was way more fun."

"You and your books." I gently tugged a lock of her soft hair. She smiled and shrugged. There was no need for either of us to mention the fact that my granddaughter devoured books as if afraid they would be taken away from her. It was one of the things I loved most about her, for in my younger years I, too, used to read every spare hour I was fortunate enough to have. It was a common bond between us, our love of literature.

"Well," I changed the subject, "I knew this would be my last chance to see you before you go back to Colorado, and I wanted to give you your graduation gift before you left."

She slid her arm through mine. "Aww, Grandpa, you don't need to give me anything. Just spending time with you is enough present for me."

"You're a sweetheart," I said as another pang of sorrow pierced me. I swallowed back the sadness and focused only on what I was about to tell her.

"But there's something I have for you that's a little bit better than just lunch with an old fellow." She snickered with disdain, which I fully appreciated. "You see," I turned us away from the house, her arm still in mine. "There's one thing I have that I know you've loved ever since I got it. And I wanted it to be your graduation present."

She tilted her head curiously, knitting her brows as if I had just asked her a difficult question she was trying to figure out the answer to. "What is it?"

I let go of her and walked around to the other side of the car, so we were standing on both sides of it. With a grin, I took out my keys and tossed them lightly over the vehicle to my granddaughter. She caught them in both hands, the look on her face plainly not registering just yet what was happening as she looked from them to me. I folded my arms and waited until it began to dawn on her. Then the excitement and joy in her beautiful eyes shone like summer sunshine through clouds. I expected a big hug, but not quite as much enthusiasm as she showered me with when she dashed around the car and threw her arms around my neck, almost knocking me over.

"I don't know how I'll ever thank you enough! I mean, I know how much you love this car and take such good care of it, and now you're just giving it to me! I can't believe it! I'm so excited, I don't know what to say! I love you so much! Oh thank you, thank you, thank you, Grandpa!"

I hugged her back and let her keep bubbling over until she had to pause to draw breath, enjoying her excitement that refreshed my old spirit. My granddaughter was college age, but she was still such a little girl in heart. Her innocence and passion soothed my soul.

"I don't deserve your car, Grandpa," she said breathlessly, finally letting go of me as she began looking over the familiar convertible with both wonder and the pride of new ownership.

"Oh yes you do," I answered firmly. "You are a wonderful granddaughter, and every one of us in the family is proud of you."

She looked at me from where she was bracing herself with her hands against the car door.

"If your grandmother were here, I know she would want

you to have it, too."

She straightened up, her face suddenly solemn. She looked down at the keys still clutched in her small hand.

"Come on," I said gently, "Let's head to lunch, and then afterward you can drop me off at my office. I'll take one of the company cars home from there."

She bounced the keys in her hand and gave me a lopsided grin.

"We aren't going to that terrible seafood place again, are we?" she asked.

"Hey, I liked it," I retorted with a laugh as she shook her head in mock exasperation. "Just remember who's paying for this joint venture."

"Right. But..." She opened the door to the driver's side. "Just remember who's driving us there!"

"You are a sly one," I said and we both chuckled as I sat down beside her in the car that used to be mine only a few minutes ago. I had no regrets. I knew I was leaving it in very capable hands.

A couple hours later, the bright red sports car pulled up to the main gate of a large campus of office buildings. I directed my granddaughter over to the booth where a security guard stepped out to inspect us. I was familiar with him, since I passed him nearly every day coming to and from work. He immediately recognized me when he peered at us through the driver's window.

"Good afternoon, Mr. Winstead. Miss," he nodded to her. She smiled back cordially while I waved my hand as he cleared us for entry. We drove through the gate and pulled into a parking space in front of the largest office building. She cut the engine but just sat there, staring straight ahead. Neither of us said a word for a few silent moments. Then she took off her seat belt and twisted to the side to look at me.

"Grandpa, I don't know how to thank you enough for this beautiful car, and for lunch...not to mention everything you've done to make it possible for me to even be able to go to college." She pushed her hair back, struggling to find the right words to express her passionate thoughts. "I haven't done anything to

deserve what you've given me."

I reached over and put my hand over hers.

"You have always been a good girl," I reassured her. She bit her lip. "I just wanted to do what I could to help you get where you want to go in life."

She nodded, her eyes focused on the dashboard.

"And you know you're my favorite granddaughter," I added sweetly, squeezing her hand.

"I'm your only granddaughter," she said smiling, but her eyes grew serious again. She looked at me intently before putting her other hand on top of mine. "I'll be back for your birthday," she said softly.

I shook my head. "No, honey. You will be so involved with your finals by that time, you don't need to worry about anything else. Let's just say our goodbyes now..." She inhaled sharply, but I continued on. "...and we'll see each other later. Ok?"

The look in her eyes shook me to the core, but I managed a steady smile when I met her gaze, keeping my tone light and matter-of-fact. She bowed up her mouth in a firm effort to keep it from trembling, but I could feel her hands shaking in mine.

"Yes," she said finally, nodding and blinking fiercely. "Yes, we will, Grandpa."

She leaned over to hug me one more time, and I felt the wetness on her cheek when it pressed against mine. I closed my eyes and held her close, silently thanking God for this precious soul I had been unbelievably blessed to call mine for twenty years.

"I love you," she whispered shakily in my ear.

"I love you too, sweetheart."

After a few more seconds, I gently let her go and opened the car door, stepping out onto the pavement while she quickly wiped her eyes and took a deep breath.

Lifting out my briefcase, I turned back to her one more time. She looked up at me with red-rimmed eyes. I put my hand on the door of her car.

"By the way, I transferred the car title, and it's in the glove box." I nodded toward it. She followed my gaze, then looked back at me. "Along with it is a prepaid card which should cover all the maintenance and gas costs for the next few years."

I stopped, feeling the slow onset of emotions I had been striving to keep in check all day. My weakening steadiness was evident in my face, and my granddaughter could see it, for I saw fresh tears fill her eyes. With great effort, I breathed deeply and then leaned down close to her.

"You have so much life to live," I said tenderly, patting her tear-streaked cheek. She tried to smile bravely. "If only I could spend more of it with you. You're such a blessing to everyone in this world, you know that?"

She lowered her head, nodding once. I kissed her forehead one last time.

"Now go on, get out of here and go live your life. You're going to do wonderful things, and God will surely be glorified through you. Remember what I've always told you?"

She sniffed a couple times before saying with a tremor in her voice, "Remember who I am, Who I belong to, and that God will always take care of those who love Him."

"Those who love Him," I repeated, nodding for emphasis. "That would include you and me. So we can know God will always be taking care of us no matter what or where we are, right?"

"Yes, Grandpa." She wiped her eyes again. "I know."

"And don't forget, I'm expecting to see you later," I reminded her. I could feel a lump forming in my throat. I knew I would soon start my own blinking marathon. "You promise me I will?"

My precious granddaughter put her hand on mine. This time her smile was true, not merely a show to mask her sadness.

"Yes, Grandpa," she promised. "You will."

Let no one say when he is tempted, "I am tempted by God"; for God cannot be tempted by evil, nor does He Himself tempt anyone. But each one is tempted when he is drawn away by his own desires and enticed. Then, when desire has conceived, it gives birth to sin; and sin, when it is full-grown, brings forth death. -James 1:13-15

Chapter 2

Retirement

She drove away slowly, turning to look back at me several times and waving wistfully. I shaded my eyes from the sudden burst of sunlight through the heavy clouds. The golden rays shone on the beautiful red-blond hair of my granddaughter and illuminated her face like a soft sunbeam of itself. A mist rose over my vision when the convertible turned the corner at last and my treasure was gone. The ache in my heart had nothing to do with the loss of my car.

I stood alone in the parking lot for a few minutes, breathing deeply and allowing the calm from my silent prayers to wash over me, composing my thoughts again. The bright sunlight was gradually sucked away behind the overcast sky, leaving the afternoon hazy and gray.

Finally, I turned around and faced the large entryway to the office building. As I looked up at the proud glass-encased structure rising up four stories, my mind played back a dusty memory of a much younger man starting up his own business in the only space he had: the garage of his home. Now, that business had blossomed into a career that five-figure people envied. I was thankful for my humble beginnings. They reminded me where I came from and the people who had helped get me on the path to corporate and financial success, but more importantly Who had handed me all those opportunities.

This will be the last time I enter this building. How incredible that such mundane routines that are a part of our daily lives, the ones we barely have to think about, can suddenly carry

so much weight when we realize they may go away.

As I stood contemplating, I heard a voice call out to me, "Good afternoon, Mr. Winstead!"

An employee was holding the front door open, resting one arm on the door bar, his blue necktie flapping in the cool breeze. He must have seen me from inside. I nodded briefly, put on a smile, and walked over to him.

"Good afternoon to you too, Adam. How are you today? How's your family?" I inquired after thanking him for getting the door for me.

"Doing well, sir, doing well, thank you." He jogged a few steps to catch up with my long strides. "All's well at home, too. My wife is expecting again, so we're all pretty thrilled about that," he told me with an ear-to-ear grin. I stopped mid-stride and clapped him on the shoulder.

"Adam, that's wonderful! Congratulations! You tell that sweet wife of yours I'm happy for you both and wish you all the best with your new little one, ok?"

Adam turned pink and stammered his thanks and a promise to relay my message, still grinning. We took the elevator up to the third floor where he and I parted ways to our separate offices. One of the female interns greeted me cheerfully when I rounded the corner.

"Good afternoon, Molly," I responded in passing. "Would you please tell Jim that I'm here and would like to see him in my office? Thanks so much."

I was looking over some messages left for me on my desk when I heard the sound of knuckles rapping against wood. I glanced up as Jim Wilson brushed past the doorjamb into the office. He was dressed as well as any good business executive should be, with his suit spotless and shoes shined to perfection. His brown hair was parted on the side, neatly combed, and his warm hazel eyes were alert. They smiled before his mouth did. I greatly admired Jim. He was one of the few who had been with me from the earliest days of the company, coming to me fresh out of college. He was my number-two guy, a shrewd businessman, a talented career holder, and a loyal friend. I knew Jim always had my back, no matter what.

"And how is our fearless commander today?" he asked, the corners of his eyes crinkling in fun as he reached out to shake my hand. I grasped his heavily, letting out a chuckle that was only half-forced.

"Oh, he's upright, I would say."

Jim's face grew guarded. "How did your appointment go?"

I smiled sadly. "I'm as good as can be expected, under the circumstances." I turned away and shuffled a few of the papers on my desk, trying to distract myself. "This is just the kind of thing that happens when you get to be my age."

Jim closed his eyes for a brief moment, bowing his head. "I'm...I'm so sorry, Malachi."

"There's nothing you can do about it," I told him kindly. "I know how you feel, and there's no need to try apologizing for something you're not responsible for in the first place."

Jim wet his lips, then came over and put his arm around my shoulders. The friendly gesture almost shook my resolve again.

"Listen, Malachi, everyone has gone out of their way to have a big party this afternoon, sort of a double celebration for your birthday and retirement," he told me softly. "We'll all be down in the warehouse in about an hour."

I appreciated his change of subject, and nodded my assent. "Have the other arrangements been made?"

Jim dropped his arm then folded both arms across his chest. "Yes. The lawyers are in the conference room, just as you requested."

"Good, well let's not keep them waiting." I started toward the door, then realized Jim was hesitating. "Jim? Something wrong?"

"It's just...are you sure you want to go through with this right now, Malachi?" His eyes were wide and serious. "You don't have to, you know. You could wait a couple more weeks."

I sighed. "I know. But I think it's just best that I get it over with now. I want to be free of cares when the time comes, you

know?"

Jim put his hand on my arm, applying pressure for only a moment as if to say what was on his heart that couldn't be spoken in words. Then the two of us silently left my office.

The conference room was empty but for two well-groomed men in matching black suits who sat across from each other at the end of the long table in the center of the room. I noticed right away the stacks of official papers in front of both of them that each was poring over, making little notes here and there with sophisticated fountain pens. When we made our entrance, they stood up, smoothing down the front of their neckties as they took a few steps away from their chairs to shake our hands. I then took a seat by them at the table as Jim pulled out a chair next to me.

"Gentlemen," I greeted them cordially in response to their professional niceties, "Have you worked out everything as we discussed?"

The lawyers exchanged glances and both nodded in affirmation. "Yes, Mr. Winstead. Everything is just as you have requested," the one on my right said to me.

The other lawyer spoke up, "All that remains is to add your signature, and those of the witnesses, of course."

I leaned forward, folded my hands and rested my elbows on the table. "And then our business will be concluded?"

"Our deal will be closed, yes."

I turned to Jim. "I'll go over the contracts. You go ask the others to come in, will you?"

Jim nodded and stood up, exiting the conference room with the stride of a man on a mission. I dropped my eyes to the small pile of papers the lawyers subtly slid under my nose. With a quiet sigh, I picked up the pen offered to me and squinted at the fine print on the first page. Even with glasses I didn't have quite the same faith in my vision that I used to.

Maybe I should have told Jim not to hurry.

I was almost completely absorbed in the process when I heard the door open, the edge of the sanded wood softly brushing the top of the fine carpet on the floor. I made myself keep my eyes on my work, continuing my reading until I reached the end of the final page. Chairs scraped back from the table as several people sat down around me. I smelled a sweet new mixture of perfume and cologne. Jim's elbow brushed lightly against mine when he resumed his seat beside me. The room was blanketed in utter silence. I didn't have to look up to know every pair of eyes were focused on me.

At last I came to the final period and sat back in my chair, folding my hands once more. I looked up at the people around me, each in turn - the woman and four men who now sat waiting for my words. Along with Jim and me, they all represented the executive board of the company, and I knew each of them well. More importantly, I trusted each one of them. All of them were professional and capable to the uttermost in their responsibilities they held within the business. I deeply appreciated their labor and dedication to the company I had worked so hard and so long to build.

I made eye contact with each board member, then slid the papers in front of me over to the lawyer on my other side. Jim quietly cleared his throat, a subtle sign that everyone was ready for me.

"Well, all of you know why we're here," I began, tracing the cool tabletop with my fingers. "Each of you has already had a chance to review these documents?"

Nods all around. "Are there any questions regarding them?"

Nothing but silence. The woman bowed her head. They all looked very sober.

"Mr. Sean?" I addressed the tall man sitting nearest to me aside from Jim or the lawyers, and he started slightly when I called his name. "Is this what you want to do? I must have the complete agreement of all board members present here."

Sean, put on the spot, rolled his wrist wordlessly and then stroked his chin before laying his hand down on the table and nodding slowly. "I am in agreement, yes."

I gave him a grateful smile and proceeded to ask each

individual the same question. All responded affirmatively in their turn, with different emotions in their eyes and voices. I thanked them all for their decision, then turned to the lawyer on my right. "Let's do this, Mr. Lawyer."

Jim and a few of the others chuckled softly at how I addressed the lawyer, but he merely quirked his lips and then stood up, placing his fingertips on the table while he spoke to the room.

"As you all know, Mr. Winstead is very generously selling the company to you, his executive board. Each of you will have an equal share, except Mr. Wilson here. He will have two shares and will serve as the president of the corporation."

I sensed Jim stir beside me. I knew what was going through his mind.

Yes, you do deserve this, old friend. More than anyone, you do.

The lawyer was still going on in his professional way.

"Mr. Winstead is selling you the company at the lowest price possible so as to stay within the law of a legal sale. Each one of you will pay for your part interest in the company each year. Now, the sum of these payments will be made payable to Mr. Winstead's foundation, which will be administrated by our office according to his wishes."

He then spread the documents out on the table and requested that the other board members come up and sign for their parts of the contract. I watched every careful curve of the ink traced on the smooth white paper until at last Jim Wilson turned from adding his signature and held the pen out to me. I took it from his hand and slid the contract in front of me.

There was no point in delaying to think anything over one last time. I signed my name with a flourish.

The first lawyer extended his hand toward the back of the room. "And now the witnesses will please add their signatures."

I hadn't even noticed the two secretaries, one my own and the other Jim's, who were sitting quietly away from the table. They must have slipped in with the others when I was still going over the contract. They now both laid down their notepads and pencils and walked over, both passing me warm smiles before signing the documents on the appropriate lines.

The second lawyer who hadn't said much during the procedure now pulled the contract over in front of him and took a couple of minutes to review it. He then looked up at me through his crystal-clear glasses. "It's done. That completes the sale."

I stood up, and immediately each of my board members rose from their chairs and came over to shake my hand, each respectfully offering a few words of praise and thanks.

"Thank you for everything you've done for this company, Malachi."

"We appreciate you so much, sir."

"You've done so much for each of us, Malachi. Thank you."

"I know I'm leaving the business in the most excellent and capable hands," I said, looking around at all the sober faces. They filed out slowly, one by one, leaving me with Jim and the lawyers.

"Gentlemen, I want to thank you both for your fine work," I told the two lawyers, who shook my hand one last time before gathering up their things and departing with a snap of their fancy briefcase clamps. I took a deep breath, suddenly feeling like a weight had been taken off my shoulders. A smile of relaxation passed over my face, and I turned to Jim.

"Did I hear you say something about a party?" I asked him jovially. He smiled.

The company warehouse was decorated with festive colored streamers, balloons, and celebration banners to create a party atmosphere. Several round tables were set up with white tablecloths draped over them, surrounded by chairs festooned with more streamers and balloons. When Jim and I entered, the huge group of people gathered there turned around and began applauding, accompanied by smiles and cheers.

I stopped at the door, overtaken by a flood of emotion. I could see there must be at least two hundred people here; not just my employees but people from other companies who were

suppliers or buyers of my company products. And they were all gathered here to celebrate me. Amazement, gratitude, and embarrassment made my face feel warm.

Jim, who had backed away from me and was also joining in the clapping, now led me over to a standing microphone. At the same time, some of the others began wheeling in a giant cake from another room toward me. When it reached me at the microphone, everyone started to sing "Happy Birthday." I stared down at the beautiful white cake with my name frosted in baby-blue letters amidst swirling designs and the pale, waxy candles, eighty-two in all. I looked around at my admiring audience, and my eyes began to water.

The singing concluded, people sat down at their tables, their eyes still intently on me standing at the microphone. I stood in silence, biting my lip in effort to hold back my emotions. In spite of the tears in my eyes, I could feel a smile coming on out of sheer warmth as I observed all those around me. The sentiment of what they had done for me was almost overwhelming. I knew as I stood there looking out on all those beaming faces that I would never forget this moment when these loving people had come together to remember me.

"I can only say to each and every one of you how important it has been to me and this company to work with each one of you," I said, the microphone humming quietly when I spoke into it. "It is your work that has made this company the worldwide success that it is today. And as this is my last day here with you, I want you all to know that I..."

I took a deep breath, steadying my trembling hands by shoving them deep in my pockets. Rocking back on my heels a bit, I blinked fiercely and went on.

"I am so thankful to my God for the great opportunity that He has given me to work with you over these many years. It's been a long journey, though rough at times." I glanced over at Jim, who was nodding with a smile on his face. "But always a joy, knowing I was working with the best people trying to make this world the best she could be with what we had to offer. You all helped make that journey better for me, personally. Thank you all."

I raised one hand and stepped away from the microphone, afraid to say more for fear of losing control. For a few moments, there was silence in the room. Then Jim, who came to meet me and vigorously shake my hand as I stepped down, began clapping as hard as he could. Others followed suit, and suddenly everyone was on their feet applauding with all their might. I nodded and tried to smile at each face I made eye contact with as I walked over to one of the tables and sat down in the place Jim indicated to me. He then took over the mic, waiting until the applause finally subsided to speak.

"Everyone, please enjoy yourselves and be sure to say a few words to Malachi this afternoon. He'll be with us for a few more hours, which should provide most of you the opportunity to personally speak to him. Because, as he said, and much more eloquently than I can, this is his last day here with us."

Here it was Jim's turn to stop and look at the ground for a moment, putting one hand on his waist and gripping the microphone stand with the other. From my seat near the front, I could see his knuckles were white. But the next instant, he raised his head, smiling once more. I was deeply moved by his affection for me, feeling that in his small display of emotion our friendship of so many years had truly reached its peak.

"The buffet line is open behind you," he gestured to a different row of tables at the back of the warehouse which were filled with trays and bowls of delicious food. "So please, go ahead and, well, eat all you want!" He shrugged his shoulders with a chuckle, and a ripple of laughter spread through the crowd.

I passed the next two hours moving through the vast number of people and trying to talk to as many of them as possible, rather than sitting and waiting for them to come to me. Everyone I spoke to greeted me as a personal friend and wished me well. Warm embraces were given all around, and more than a few friendly words were spoken about both the hard times and the good times shared by all of us who had been part of the company over the years. Every now and then, somebody approached the microphone

and said something about me that touched my old heart and filled me with gratitude. They all expressed the sentiment of how much I was loved and respected, how much I would be missed, and how thankful they were to have known me. Sometimes people simply said, "God bless you, Malachi," and it was enough. Listening to all these heartfelt remarks, I felt my life couldn't be more blessed, and my cup was running over. However, all this attention and praise directed toward me made my face heat, and, grateful as I was, being at the center of the spotlight was never something I wanted for too long. But I acknowledged each speaker with a smiling nod and a wave.

As I continued through the crowd, I began to hear not only about how much I would be missed and shared anecdotes, but people started reminding me of how much I had helped them over the years in various ways. These stories I must have forgotten, but there seemed to be many more of them than I had anticipated. The embarrassment came back, and I managed to reply to these ardent souls, "Don't thank me, thank the Lord. He's the One Who makes all things possible."

And so the time passed pleasantly, full of quiet contentment until the party began winding down at last. It was late in the afternoon when many of the guests started making their departures. Nearly all of them stopped by my table to say something to me one more time before the goodbyes. I had never shaken so many hands or given so many hugs in one day before, but I had no trouble in doing so. I loved all their love, for it reminded me of God.

Almost everyone had left when Jim Wilson walked up to me. He had his coat slung over his arm and his hat in the same hand. I stood up from my table again and reached out to him. Jim put down his things and quickly pulled me into a firm hug that meant more to me than any I had received at the party.

"I don't know what we're going to do without you, brother," he said in my ear, his voice trembling. I pulled back and held him at arm's length, smiling kindly at him.

"Jim, you just live your life for God. That's all that matters, more than this company. You do that, and I'll be the happiest you can make me, alright?"

Jim's eyes were red, but his face was calm. "You've taught me everything, you know."

"Everything I know about truth and life comes from the Bible, Jim." I put my hands on his shoulders. "You keep studying that and growing in it."

Jim nodded, swallowing hard. He managed a small smile.

"Then I'll see you later, ok?"

"Malachi..." he shook his head slightly, took a deep breath, and looked me in the eye. "Yes, I certainly hope so."

"So do I," I told him. He took my hand in both of his, squeezed gently, then let go and picked up his coat and hat. He walked away without looking back. I saw his shoulders hunch and his head dip down. My heart ached again.

Why are they called 'goodbyes'? I thought sadly. They've never been 'good' whenever I've had to say them.

I sat down in my chair once more. Nearly everyone had gone except a few staff members who remained behind to clean up around the buffet area, so I was virtually alone with my thoughts. A crumpled streamer lay across a plastic plate with a half-eaten piece of cake on it next to me. I toyed with it absently, trying to regain my composure and sift through the events of the day. A soft papery swish caught my ear. I looked over and saw the banner arched over the microphone had fallen from one of its fasteners and was now pathetically hanging by a corner. "Happy Birthday Malachi, and Congratulations on Your Retirement!" swung on end against the wall.

I watched the banner dangle there, wondering when the other string would snap, when somebody's hand pulled out a chair adjacent to mine and sat down with me at the table. I turned to see my long-time secretary, Rosemary Lark.

Rosemary was one of the most elegant women I had ever known and had always reminded me of the actresses from the golden Hollywood era. She never acted or moved about in a way that indicated she was nearly seventy, but rather always displayed a demeanor of grace, beauty, and timeless class. Her oval face was

shaped by her soft, white-blond hair, and her light blue eyes shone like jewels when she smiled. Her eyes reminded me of Vicki. Vicki's eyes used to light up like that, too.

Rosemary placed both hands on the table and instead of looking at me, looked around the room at the now-empty tables and tired decorations that had served their purpose. She sighed. It wasn't a weary sigh, or an unhappy one, but more thoughtful instead.

"You know, Malachi," she said softly, without looking at me, "All these people who came today, they were all here because they love you. And there are still many more who weren't here who love you and care for you."

I studied her, still twirling the streamer in my fingers, wondering why she was still here when all the others had gone.

"And do you know why that is? Why so many people care about you?" She finally turned in her chair to look directly at me, resting her cheek on her hand and leaning her elbow on the table. "It's because you're a good man, and they know it. Anyone who knew you for even a short time would know it." She scooted her chair a little closer to mine, and her kind face grew more serious. "But I know even more about you than many of your other employees do. I know you're a Christian, and a true one. I have always known you to be a man of your word, a man who put doing what was right first. I saw those people today who came up to you and told you how much you've helped them in the past. But so many don't know half of what you've actually done to help your employees, and others, without anyone else even knowing."

I wove the streamer slowly around my hand, thinking how to answer her. I still wasn't sure what she was here to tell me.

"Rosemary, you know I've depended on you a lot throughout the years. Much of what's been done wouldn't have happened without your help." I wadded the pastel paper into a little ball and tossed it across the table. It bounced against a clear plastic punch cup. I leaned toward Rosemary and reached out my hand. "You've been more than a good secretary; you've been a good friend."

She took my hand and gave me a half-smile. I shook her hand a little, then dropped my eyes. "You kept me and the office together for a long time after Vicki...after Vicki–"

"She was one of my closest friends," Rosemary said quietly. "It was the least I could do to help. After all, you did so much for me and my children when Bruce was killed in that hunting accident."

"Well, Rosemary, we're meant to be of help to each other through the tough times in this life. Bearing one another's burdens is a commandment given to us by God."

We sat in silence for a moment, our hands slowly falling apart until we were both just sitting there at the table in that large, empty warehouse, each thinking about similar things. Rosemary picked up the ball of crumpled paper I had tossed away and rolled it between her fingers. She seemed to be working hard in her mind to find something to say...or how to say what she had come for in the first place.

"Malachi," she said at last, her face twisting uncomfortably, "I'm not sure how to ask you this, but I do have a…a favor I would ask of you."

I looked at her inquiringly. Rosemary wasn't one to ask for much of anybody, only when she was in great need of something she couldn't do for herself, which, in her case, was rare. Wondering what her request might be, I answered, "Sure, Rosemary. I can try, anyway. What do you need?"

She twisted her hands together and brought them up to her mouth, closing her eyes for a moment and inhaling deeply. I could tell she had something pressing on her heart, and asked again, "What is it?"

Putting her hands back down on the table, she bit her lips and then said slowly, "Malachi, when you get to Heaven, will you take a message to my Bruce for me?"

I sat back, stunned. I had no idea how to answer the question she just asked of me.

"What do you mean, Rosemary?"

She leaned forward earnestly, her voice almost pleading.

"Malachi, you know Bruce was a good, faithful man. You know he loved the Lord. The morning he was killed..." She faltered, a tear starting to run down her cheek. "We...we had been having a fuss over something, right before he left. Just some little thing that didn't matter. I don't even remember what it was today. But, when Bruce left, we didn't even say goodbye to each other."

I folded my arms, focusing intently on her face, the way her words sounded as they tumbled out of her. I wanted to help her, but I didn't know how. She had stopped again, brushing her hand under her eyelashes and looking off away from me, trying to control her emotions.

"All I ask," she said, "is that you please tell him I love him. Very...very much." Her face turned redder with each word, and she finally put her head in her hands and started to cry.

My mind was boggled by the nature of her request, and still more amazing was the choice she had made in coming to me with it. What were the ramifications? How could I know I would be able to carry out such a favor, even for somebody I cared about? How should I respond?

I was thinking so hard and so fast that I forgot the poor lady sitting next to me was still in tears. I quickly realized my insensitivity and reached over to cover one of her hands with my own.

"Rosemary...I have, well, no idea if I will even be capable of giving such a message to Bruce for you," I said slowly, still in wonder over what she had asked of me. She gazed up at me, her free hand pressed against her mouth. "But, if I can, I will."

She nodded, wiping away her tears. "Thank you, Malachi. I know you will."

I squeezed her hand and then we both stood up at the same time. She stepped over to me and gave me a long, silent hug. Just before she broke away, she whispered in my ear, "I'll miss you."

Chapter 3

The Wayward Son

The few people who hadn't attended the party stopped me by ones and twos on my way out to say goodbye. I knew all their faces, even the ones to whom I might only say one or two sentences a day. But I had had enough interaction with all of them to feel a prick of the heart when we exchanged farewells. How easy it is to grow accustomed to another's face, and then when in a short time they disappear...the emptiness is startling.

I took one of the company cars home from the office. Parking in the driveway, I stepped out of the car and walked over to the mailbox at the curbside. The painted, shapeless murals swirling over the postal box that were once bright had now faded and turned gray. I ran my hand along the side of the mailbox, pausing to rest it against the handprint of a child beside the lowered red flag. Each of my grandchildren had left a piece of their personalities on this mailbox in the form of painted handprints. It made my heart smile every time I went to check my mail.

"Malachi, hey, Malachi!"

I drew out the thin stack of commercial fliers and envelopes, closing the metal door with a loud squeal that protested of rust and corrosion. Turning around, I saw one of my neighbors, Dike Randal, waving at me from his lawn a couple doors down. I raised one hand to wave back, and he started over to me. Wondering what he wanted, I tucked my mail under my arm and waited, leaning one hand against the mailbox post.

I had gotten to know Dike and his wife fairly well over the past few years they had lived on my street. Dike read gas meters for a living when he had first come here, and he and I met when he came to read the neighbor's meter across the street from my house and was chased by their dog into my yard. I had been in the garage repairing my grandson's bike and saw the excitement unfolding, dimly recognizing this man as my newest neighbor. I quickly ushered him through the garage door and into the house, where I got him some ice water and we began to visit while he recovered from his ordeal. I kept one eye on the snarling mastiff through the window until it finally stalked away. I had never liked that dog, but after that episode I realized the unfriendly animal had been a means to making a new friend. Dike and I often stopped to visit with each other after that, and they had me over for dinner a few times. They also had a couple of children who had left home before I'd met Dike and his wife, but when I was with them they didn't speak much about their kids.

Dike walked up to me now and stuck out his hand. I shook it with a smile, noting that instead of his usual firm handshake, he took my hand in both of his and held it almost as if he was afraid he would break it.

"Afternoon, Dike."

"Afternoon, Malachi." His tone was somewhat softer than usual, very kind and caring. I only had two seconds to be puzzled by his gentle attitude before he followed up with, "How are you doing?"

Ah, more sympathy for the inevitable. I sighed internally. I wish I didn't have to be constantly reminded, but then I knew that Dike only meant to show concern. I could appreciate that.

"Thanks, Dike, I'm well enough as it is. I have my good days and bad days, you know. But how are you and Louise doing?" I quickly changed the subject.

"Doing fine, doing fine." He braced himself against the chain-link fence beside my mailbox, leaning on his elbow with his arms crossed. "Louise went to be with her mother after the knee surgery last week, so it's just me fending for myself at the house."

"Uh-oh, I hope you're surviving."

"Barely," he grinned and ran a hand back through his

bristly hair that grayed at the temples, though I knew he had not yet reached fifty. Knowing Dike and what he had gone through in his life, however, there wasn't much curiosity in my mind as to why his hair was turning gray.

"Well, how's business at your store?" Dike had started his own business several months after we had met.

"It's always good during the fall months when everybody's out buying firearms for hunting," he answered proudly. I knew how much pride he took in the gun business he ran. If ever there was a man more enamored with lead-spitting weaponry than Dike, I had yet to meet him.

The conversation waned after this, and we both stood in a somewhat awkward silence that reminded me of sitting with my secretary, Rosemary, earlier. Wanting to get back into the quiet of my own home, I glanced off down the street, then at the letters in my hand, thinking maybe Dike didn't have much more to say and would say "so long" and be off. Instead, he cleared his throat.

"Uh, Malachi, do you have a minute?"

I looked up. "Sure, Dike. What's going on?"

He lifted his shoulders up almost to his ears, shoving his hands deep into his pockets. "Well, I want to ask you about something."

"Alright, sure. Here, let's go on up to the house and we can visit, ok?"

He nodded vigorously, giving a smile that displayed to my perception mainly relief. Had he been afraid I would say no to his request for a moment of my time? Dike and I were more friendly than most neighbors are with each other. We had shared our lives with each other one cup of coffee or icy soda at a time. His discomfort now in speaking to me caused the curiosity to well up in my brain, but I figured I would wait it out until he was ready to tell me, as he evidently wanted to.

On the wrap-around porch, I put my mail on the railing and invited Dike to take a seat on one of the white wicker chairs. "Can I get you something to drink? Coffee? Water?"

Dike dropped into the chair and leaned forward with his

hands folded between his knees. "No thanks, I'm fine."

I sat down across from him, adjusting the thin, weathered pillow at my back.

"So, Dike, what can I do for you?" I asked.

He rubbed his hands back and forth a moment before clasping them together tightly again. "Malachi, you remember about my son Josh?"

I bowed my head, nodding sadly. "Yes. I was very sorry to hear of your loss, Dike. I've been praying for you and Louise ever since."

He shifted in his seat, staring at his entwined hands. "Yeah, he was always a good kid, Josh." He took a deep breath to steady himself. Then he threw himself back in his chair, folding his arms across his chest, cocking his head as he stared into space. "He'd never been in trouble of any kind, kept his grades up, stuck to the rules, you know." A thoughtful frown formed between Dike's eyebrows. He looked back up at me. "When Josh was twenty years old, he told Louise and me that he wanted to move out and live in San Francisco. Now, why he wanted to live there, I'll never know." Dike let out a short chuckle that sounded more desperate than funny. He struggled to keep his emotions from showing through as he spoke, and my heart ached for him.

"Well, anyway, he did move to San Francisco, and while he was there he got mixed up with the wrong people who influenced him for the worse. Long story short, my son wound up dying of AIDS." Dike flipped his hand as if to wave away the past, but I could see the pain in his eyes. He had never told me this part of the story.

"When we heard he was in the hospital, his mother and I went to see him. It was only hours between our getting there and the time that he died. He was unconscious before we got a chance to speak to him." Dike swallowed hard and turned his head away.

I reached forward and put a hand on his arm.

"I'm truly sorry, Dike." My voice shook. "I can't begin to imagine the tragedy you've gone through, how hard it must be to lose a child like you and Louise have."

He merely shook his head, running his tongue over his lips and blinking rapidly. Then he turned to me, his voice full of pleading.

"Malachi, I wanted to ask you that, if, well, when you...pass over to the next place, maybe you could give my son a message? Because we didn't get to really tell him goodbye?"

The strange sensation of déjà vu passed over me like a cloud across the sun. Two such requests in one day! Once again, a sense of helplessness and bewilderment crowded my thoughts. What on earth was I possibly supposed to say? Why was I even being asked such a thing? I looked at Dike, at this man who had become my friend. I thought about what he had told me of his son, Josh. And suddenly, the truth cut through the leaping chaos in my brain and, like the clearest of bells, tolled an answer for me to give my neighbor. I knew what I had to tell him could not bring the comfort he so desperately sought. But as much as the truth hurt, I had to say what was right. Dike had given me no choice, and it was he who had come to me to hear what I could tell him. He had a right to know.

"Dike," I said slowly, trying to think through every word I was about to say to this heartbroken man. "I'm very, very sorry. I wish I could give that message to your son for you. I know you loved him very much."

Dike stared at me, not comprehending my subtle signs of warning.

"But I have to tell you, Dike," I hesitated, "from what you have told me about your son, I don't think he'll be where I'm going. I won't be able to pass your words along to him."

I knew the anger was coming, but I didn't expect Dike to jump up, almost knocking his chair over.

"What do you mean he won't be where you're going?" he demanded harshly, his eyes flashing.

"I'm sorry, Dike!" I repeated, feeling like a broken record that brought futile alleviation. "I'm only trying to be truthful with you."

Dike looked around wildly, then turned around and pressed

his hands against the porch railing, bowing his head down low and shaking it in disbelief. I stood up behind him.

"Dike, you're my friend. You need to know the truth."

He whirled back to face me, his eyes red.

"So what you're telling me is that my son is going to hell?" His words were razor-edged. I opened my mouth, but he cut me off. "Well, I'm telling you that Josh was a good kid and a good son! If he was different, it was because he was born that way! If he got mixed up with bad people, he couldn't help that! Circumstances were beyond his control!"

I backed away from his fury, but kept my hand outstretched toward him in supplication.

"Dike, again, I'm sorry. Only God judges those things."

This time I almost expected him to maybe throw a chair and storm off the porch, but instead he walked up close to me, so close I could see the tears welling up in his eyes. He pointed a finger in my face and gritted his teeth.

"You should be the one going to hell for saying that," he hissed, a tear spilling down his cheek. "God loves everyone! And I know this, that my son will not be where you should go!"

"Dike," I pleaded, "I told you, I can only tell you the truth. God gives us all a free will, and we choose how we spend our lives, either in service to Him or in slavery to sin. But what we do when we're alive here on earth has a voice after our souls have passed on."

I prayed my words carried some small weight with Dike, but he was deaf to my entreaty to reason. He backed away from me, his feet stumbling as he made his way back down the porch steps. His watery eyes were still fixed on me with a look of hatred that pained me deeply.

"My son was good," he repeated fiercely, dashing away another tear with his fist. "No matter what you say, in my heart," and he stabbed a finger at his chest, "I know he is in heaven! And if there is a hell, I hope you find yourself there!"

I closed my eyes as Dike stalked away, sinking down into my chair again. A door slammed a short way down the street a minute later, ending a relationship. I thought about what he had said to me. I thought about Rosemary too. Both of their supplications had been born of grief and a longing to heal that incomplete part of their hearts that had been doubly wounded under the weight of being unable to say goodbye to the ones they loved before they were taken away. They had both come to me hoping for the smallest degree of comfort in knowing that the last words to their loved ones they had been unable to say might be passed along by other means. One person had received that comfort, the other only more pain. I let my head fall against the back of my chair, letting out a full sigh.

How the truth can cut like a sword.

The funeral home was ornate, but in a subdued way, as if the stiff, luxurious furniture, stained glass, and crowds of plants and flowers were themselves in mourning for the deceased. The atmosphere upon entering immediately hushed any idea of conversation into a whisper.

I passed through the wave of black-garbed folks, friends and family of the departed soul we were all there to memorialize today. Some were talking, some were dabbing their eyes with tissues, others stood in silence while others around them even smiled from time to time in remembrance of happy times with their beloved friend.

Some of the more worldly-minded would find this odd of me, but I for one had always found a strange comfort in attending funerals. They helped me keep my perspective in place, and reminded me of the value of life, and what a blessing a single life well lived can be. And in my many years, I had been at the funerals of many a dear friend and loved one, drawing strength from their courageous legacies and thanking God that I would see many of them again one day. Funerals had taught me long ago how short life is, and reminded me what was truly important. And, after all, how could I not be encouraged by attending a funeral where I knew the person had gone on to a far better place? The grief was there and it was sharp, but at least there was also the comfort of knowing that soul was now safely on the other side.

I made my way to a seat in the chapel area, but before I could get there I was repeatedly stopped by several folks I knew. Each greeted me with a hearty handshake or hug. They all wished me well as if they were there to celebrate my life instead of the good lady we were all actually here for.

It feels as if they all know this might be the last time most of them will see me.

As the funeral began, there were prayers offered, songs sung, and many sweet words spoken for the friends and family. I felt my own eyes growing moist as I fixed them on the shiny wooden casket down at the front, well-surrounded by a foliage of leaves and flowers. I had known this woman. Her name was Maria Stiles. She had been a fine lady and a hard worker in the church. We used to attend the same congregation to worship every week for many years before her health had steadily declined with age. I remembered she used to teach the children's Bible class, as well as fix food for, and visit, the sick and shut-ins. If ever there was a need in the church, she was there to fill it. Her sunny disposition and giving spirit had always exhorted everyone around her, myself included.

My eyes drifted down to one of the figures sitting on the front pew nearest to the preacher speaking beside the coffin. From where I sat, I could see the side of the man's face who sat hunched over his clasped hands, his head bowed while several strands of gray-brown hair fell down across his forehead. As I watched in sympathy, his shoulders started to shake from time to time until he could regain control of his emotions.

Walter, if only you knew the truth. Then you could be sure of seeing her again.

Walter Stiles, Maria's husband and now widower, was not a Christian. In fact, he was a self-proclaimed atheist who would have nothing to do with the church or any kind of religious belief. The Stiles were well off, and he was a highly respected lawyer in the city. I don't know what it was in his life that made him deny the existence of God, but I struggled almost even more trying to understand how two people so stridently opposite in their beliefs could be so caring toward one another like Walter and Maria. As far as I knew, their marriage had been one of great happiness, in spite of their conflicting world views.

She must have tried to help him see, I thought. She must have begged him to come to church, to study the Bible with her, to just learn the Gospel and see the truth for himself. What kind of marriage would that be like? Even when two people truly love each other, the struggle must put a strain there.

The funeral came to an end, and the casket was carried out to the waiting hearse. As if on cue, the sky began to shed drops of rain that gradually turned into a torrential downpour when folks were leaving. Because of the rain, only a few made it out to the cemetery for the graveside service. The small green pavilion adjacent to the burial spot offered little room with only a few chairs. I stood at the back, feeling the rain dripping down the back of my coat collar that was exposed to the weather. I noticed Walter again, seated at the front of the two short rows of chairs, his head in his hands. I hadn't gotten a chance to speak to him with so many surrounding him for comfort at the funeral home. I resolved to say a few words to him before we all left the grave site.

The preacher opened his Bible and began to speak, but my thoughts slowly turned to the inevitable subject that standing here among these tombs was pulling to the front of my mind again—my death. Soon it would be my body lying there in a shining casket like this one, surrounded by flowers, friends, and family all gathered in a cemetery like this one. I saw a beautiful girl with long red hair against her black dress, with tears running down her sweet face, and swallowed at the lump in my throat. But at the same time I knew. I knew it would only be my body lying there in that wooden box placed in the cold earth. By the time my funeral took place, my soul, the essence of who I was, would be long gone. I would be home at last, like Maria Stiles.

The graveside service was short and ended with the pallbearers solemnly placing their boutonnieres on the lid of the coffin before it was lowered into the waiting ground. Everyone stopped to offer their condolences once more to Walter before passing by me to go back to their vehicles in the rain. I moved to the side to make room, hovering near the back corner of the tent until nearly all the guests had gone. The preacher was the last one to take Walter's hand, leaning down and whispering in his ear. I saw Walter nod mutely. The preacher clasped his shoulder before slowly walking away, giving me a nod when he saw me.

The funeral director who was also there opened his black umbrella and motioned to Walter that he would help him back to the funeral limousine. I stepped forward, determined to say something to him before he left. Walter indicated "not yet" to the director. The other man closed his umbrella and sat down at the end of the row of chairs to give the grieving husband a few more moments with his deceased wife.

The longer I watched him, the more I marveled. Walter stood up and just stood there, staring at the closed coffin of his beloved wife. Then he walked up to it and pressed his hand against the cool wood, crushing one of the flowers scattered across it. He just couldn't let go. How could he, not believing in any kind of life after death? For him, he had lost his soul mate forever and would never see her again. I could imagine he felt both loss and terror right now, and my heart ached for him all the more. How awful to live a life having no idea what waits beyond the grave, nothing but a yawning pit of blackness, of unconsciously ceasing to exist. No wonder Walter was desperately trying to cling to something that once gave him a reason worth living for, but could now no longer help him.

But maybe somebody else could.

I took my chance and walked softly around the chairs until I was standing beside him. Without saying a word, I just let myself be there with him, let him know another human being was there and that they cared about him. Walter was balling his fists at his sides now, but suddenly he spoke and his voice was calm.

"I don't believe in your God, the God Maria believed in, or any other," he said hoarsely. A tear ran down his cheek. He wiped it roughly away. I didn't say anything, letting the hurt work its way through him.

"Twenty years ago," he said, almost as if he were talking to himself, "Your God took her from me. She started believing in Him, and He became first in her life. Not me, Him. Our life together was never the same after that." Walter shook his head. He still wouldn't look at me. He spoke as if to the rain and the gravestones. "I, I hated your God even more. I tried hard for years to keep her away from the church. But it seemed like the more I tried, the more committed to Him she became. She had changed. There were things she would no longer do. She would say things like, 'I can't do that. It would be a sin.'"

"The life of a Christian is a different one than most people understand," I said carefully, placing a hand on his shoulder. He glanced at me, then almost smirked. His eyes were glassy. He pulled away from me, walking to stand at the edge of the tent alongside the coffin. Gripping one of the tent poles, he faced away from me, though I could see his jaw working as if he had more to say.

"One night I'd been drinking," he said finally, his voice low. "I was nearly drunk, too. I told her she had to choose, that it would have to be me or her precious God. I said if she kept going to church, she would have to leave. And she just left the room and went to bed. She didn't say a word." He slowly turned around, his face incredulously sorrowful. He looked as if he had discovered a terrible truth that he didn't understand. "I remember the look on her face...I knew I had really hurt her in that moment. But I didn't care. I had drunk so much and was so angry..." Walter bowed his head, biting his lip. "I didn't care. And the next morning, she was gone. It took me weeks to find her, and days to convince her that I was sorry and would never act that way again. So for twenty years now, I never said another word about her God or the church. And now..." Walter's shoulders started shaking again as his eyes screwed up to fight back tears. "Now I've lost her forever."

I quickly put an arm around his shoulders, seizing the opportunity to help. "No, Walter. You're wrong. Maria isn't gone forever. She simply has gone on, to a place where she is happy and would only be happier if she knew you were coming to meet her there, too. It's a more wonderful place than any we can imagine or know. We can't even understand what it's like where your wife is now, but I know it is a perfect place. And Walter," I added, giving him a comforting little shake, "I will see her there soon."

"How do you know that?" he asked brokenly.

I smiled. "Because God has told us all that He gave up. His own Son was a sacrifice so that one day we might live with them both in heaven. And in heaven, Walter, there will be no more pain, no more tears, no more sorrow, and no more goodbyes in the rain. No goodbyes ever. Because those who love God will finally all have come home."

He looked back at his wife's coffin. I couldn't tell what was going through his mind other than the heart-stricken grief still clawing his face.

"You can be with her again, Walter. I promise you can, if only you would believe and do what God has asked every one of us to do. And He never gives us more than we can bear. Let your wife's legacy make you stronger. Let her example help guide you toward God, and in doing so you honor her in a better way than you could ever do."

He was still looking at the casket, his head bowed. Then he turned to me. His voice was heavy as he said quietly, "Goodbye, Malachi. It's all over."

He then slowly walked from the shelter of the tent out into the rain with the funeral director hurrying along behind him, opening his umbrella to hold it over Walter's head.

Three days later, I was watching the evening news when a news alert sprang up that one of the most successful and recently widowed lawyers in Seattle had died suddenly of an apparent suicide, though an investigation was being carried on to make sure of the details. I didn't have to guess who the victim was.

If only he would have sought help and tried to follow the truth himself. He and Maria could have been together forever.

Chapter 4

The Gas Station

I stood at the gas pump, my finger tight around the nozzle trigger as I filled up my car. I might have given away my glistening red sports car to my granddaughter, but that didn't mean I had no other vehicles. The car I had driven into town today was a jet black Porsche with gleaming silver hubcaps on the dustless tires. It was my second favorite car, because it was the one in which I had taught my oldest grandchild to drive in. Now it carried a week's worth of groceries in the back seat.

As I stood there, musing vaguely to myself over the skyrocketing prices in gasoline, I heard somebody call my name. I craned my neck to see into the next lane over and saw a middle-aged woman standing beside a silver minivan waving at me. She looked somewhat familiar...

"Mr. Malachi! It's me, Stacy! Stacy Landow!"

Ah, yes, I remembered her now. Stacy had once worked for me as a phone receptionist a few years ago before moving on to another job. We hadn't spoken much during her time at the company or after she left, but I smiled and waved back to her.

"Hey, after you fill up, pull over there, will you?" She circled her hand at a vacant parking space a few yards away. "I need to talk to you!"

I hadn't seen her in at least two years. I couldn't imagine what she wanted to talk about, but I nodded to indicate I would do as she asked. I was still filling up when I saw she finished and pulled over into one of the empty spaces. I was done a few seconds later and soon pulled up beside her.

I'll just see what she has on her mind.

Being parked on the passenger side of her car, I rolled down the driver's side window, but to my surprise, she opened her car door and came around both our vehicles. She opened the passenger door to my car and sat down next to me. Without missing a beat, she held out her hand for me to shake.

To say I was startled was an understatement, but I managed a polite smile and gently shook hands with her. A moment later, she was waving a small white card under my nose. She certainly didn't waste any time getting started.

"Mr. Malachi, after I left the company, I got into real estate," she informed me. "And I think I'm doing quite well. The business is successful if you're driven enough to pursue it, and I know I am." She laughed boisterously.

"Well, good. I'm glad things are going well for you, Stacy." I looked down at the card.

She nodded several times rapidly, but then slower and slower. Finally, a tiny frown crept over her face. Suddenly, she scooted a few inches closer to me. I leaned back out of instinct, unprepared for her sudden movement.

"Mr. Malachi," she said seriously, "you remember my good friend, Alice Clark?"

"Ah..." I wracked my brain. "She's in accounting at the company."

"Yes. She told me you sold your business."

"She's right." I offered no further explanation.

Stacy studied me thoughtfully for a moment, blinking her heavily shadowed eyes before looking straight ahead through the windshield. "Alice told me why, too."

It was my turn to look out the window now. I could feel her looking at me again and closed my eyes in a deep exhale.

"I just want you to know how very sorry I am to hear about your...situation." She cleared her throat nervously. "How...how are you doing? Are you, you know, feeling ok and all that?"

I gave her a real smile this time. What was the point of being downcast? It wouldn't help anyone or anything. "Thanks, Stacy. I'm doing alright. So many people have been very kind to me, and I'm a blessed man."

She pushed her tongue against her upper lip, then said, "Well, I just want you to know that ever since I heard, I've been praying for you every day. I've asked my church to pray for you, too."

"That's very kind of you, Stacy. Thank you."

She relaxed back into her seat, satisfied, but only for a second before bolting forward again, which in turn made me jump slightly as before.

"Malachi, this may not be the best time to ask, but, like I said, I am in the real estate business, and if you need to sell your home quick I can certainly turn that beautiful house of yours into cash," she said. "I know people who are looking for a house like yours, and I can get you top dollar!"

"Eh, no thanks, Stacy. My home isn't for sale. It goes to my estate."

Is this all she wanted to talk about? I could feel myself growing antsy. I had a lot to do and so little time in which to do it...

"Oh, well, that's ok. Just take my card, alright? In case you change your mind, or somebody comes to you wanting to buy the house." She tapped it with a bright red fingernail.

I tried to politely end the conversation by agreeing to take her card with me and then looking out the windows and nodding as if the conversation was finished. The subject matter was making me both uncomfortable and sad, not to mention just a little irritated with how callous this woman sounded when talking about the affairs I would have to put in order, even if she didn't mean to be that way.

Stacy had grown suddenly quiet, biting her lip. Then she gently swatted my arm with the back of her hand and said, "Hey, while I have you here, can I ask you a question?"

I sighed internally. She probably wanted to ask if I knew of any other prospective house sellers in my area. "Yes, what is it?"

"Do you remember my brother, DJ?"

The question took me aback. I shook my head. "I can't say that I do."

"That's alright," she answered quickly. "He worked one summer at your company, helping out in the shipping department. That was just a few months before he went into the army."

"Well, Stacy, it's a pretty big company with lots of people. Unfortunately, I wasn't able to personally get to know everybody there." I fiddled with my key ring.

"I understand..." she paused, then said in a rush, "my brother was killed last summer from a roadside bomb in Iraq."

I immediately regretted growing frustrated with her, and sympathy washed over me. "Oh, Stacy, I'm truly sorry for your loss. We should always be grateful to, and for, those who give their lives and safety to defend our country."

She bowed her head and nodded in acceptance of my condolences. Then she looked up and determinedly met my eyes. "You're a Christian, Mr. Malachi. And I know you won't be with us much longer. Can I ask you to do something special for me?"

I was starting to get that distinct feeling of déjà vu again. "What did you have in mind, Stacy?"

"When you cross over, will you tell my brother, DJ, that we all miss him? For me?"

"Ah..." I had begun to hope this would not be the kind of 'help' she was looking for. Once again, I was left surprised and confused as I dangled between a flat, straight answer and a wobbly promise that I wasn't sure was mine to make.

"Was your brother a faithful Christian?" I asked, grasping for more information while I dithered.

"Oh yes!" she said eagerly. "DJ and I were both born-again Christians when we were teenagers."

"But was DJ ever baptized for the remission of his sins?"

I saw the confusion in her eyes, and my heart sank.

"No," her answer was slow. "We were never baptized. We were simply saved."

"Then I'm afraid I can't make that promise, Stacy. I'm so sorry, but I will not be going where your brother is."

It pained my heart when anger leaped into her expression. Then, just as quickly, it faded and she bent her head as she began to cry. "How do you know that?" she pleaded between sobs.

"Stacy, if your brother never obeyed God according to what one must do to be saved, then he won't be in paradise. I'm sorry."

How many times can I say that, and how much sorrier is God over every sinner who dies lost?

She was looking at me hard now. "How can you say that about my brother? He was always a good boy and a good man. He helped anybody in need and would give you the shirt off his back! He and the young people from church would take food to the hungry during the holidays. He taught Sunday school and sang in the choir..." She was getting more and more keyed up, her face turning red. "He served Jesus any and every way he could! Why are you telling me he won't be in heaven?"

"Stacy, I'm not trying to hurt you because I tell you the truth. Please believe me. I'm not condemning anyone. The Lord alone has said who will and who will not be saved, and the ones who will be are those who follow Him according to His will in the Bible..."

I trailed off as she put her hands over her face and cried as though her heart would break. Feeling utterly helpless as how to console her but at the same time wanting to be of some comfort, I reached out to put my hand on her shoulder to show I cared about her and her sad situation. But she shrugged away from me, opening the car door with one hand and dashing away tears with the other. Slamming the door behind her, she marched around to her car and sped off, almost hitting another vehicle. Yet again, I was reminded how truth can hurt so much. The scenarios I had encountered during the past week had both astounded me and gave me cause to wonder. Both sorrow and hope had been the outcome of my responses to the promises these souls had asked me to make, and still I didn't know why they were coming to me.

Why, Lord, do people keep asking me to help them in this way? Is there some way You will use me through this?

I sat in the parking space a few more minutes, until I realized that I needed to get home pretty soon or my ice cream in the back seat was going to melt.

A few days later I received a phone call from my son, Garrett.

"Hey, Dad! Why don't you come over for dinner tonight?" he offered.

I hadn't seen him and his wife in over a week and accepted his invitation with enthusiasm. I got an idea to stop by the nearest market store and see if I could find a carton of eggnog to take along to my son's house. I knew it was a stretch, but I hoped maybe there might be an early batch this season. It was the only way I would get to drink any this year. Eggnog was my favorite drink, after coffee.

But it wasn't to be. I wandered up and down the aisles, then asked a store associate for assistance, but all in vain. Early October is just too early for eggnog.

So none for me this year, I thought wistfully. The simple triviality of missing out on my special drink because I had gone searching for it too early seemed more bitter in light of why I couldn't have any more of it. In efforts to soothe my disappointment, I bought another gallon of Blue Bell Rocky Road ice cream. I would take that over to my son's house for dinner instead.

Upon leaving the store, I had almost made it back to my car when I saw an older couple approaching from the other side. They were clearly headed straight for me, both smiling and waving at me. The faces looked familiar, and then I recognized them as they drew closer. A smile broke out over my own face. Shifting my grocery bag to the other hand, I reached out toward the gentleman.

"Hey, Miguel! I thought it was you!" I exclaimed appreciatively as he clasped my hand.

"Malachi Winstead, it is good to see you again," he told me heartily. "It's been quite a while."

"Too long," I agreed, turning to give the woman a gentle hug. "Maria, it's a joy to see you looking so well."

"And to see you, Malachi," she said, her voice sweet.

"Well, how have you two been?" I leaned against my car

door, giving the ice cream bag a little swing. "I don't think we've spoken face-to-face since you retired, Miguel."

He chuckled and put an arm around his wife. "Yes sir, that was nearly two years ago. We moved south shortly after I left the company and have been doing pretty well."

"We have been helping our youngest son and his wife," Maria put in. "They started a printing business in Salem, and we have been working with them."

"And we've been meaning to come by the office to thank you," Miguel added, "for the wonderful card and flowers that you...that you and the company sent for our grandson's funeral." He stopped, suddenly overcome by emotion. I nodded sympathetically. Such a wound never fully heals; neither time nor circumstance can change that.

"There's no need to thank me," I told the couple. "It was my honor to do what I could in such a terrible time for you, my friends. I know you loved your grandson very much."

Maria's eyes were swimming with tears. "It was such a horrible accident. He had drowned in my son's swimming pool. He was only three and could not swim."

"I can't imagine what you're going through," I said sincerely, wishing I had better words of encouragement. "I was out of the country at the time, or I would have come to the funeral. I truly regret not being able to be there. I was thinking of you and the rest of your family during the time."

They looked at me with grateful, though teary eyes. "We know, Mr. Malachi," Maria said with passion. "And we thank you so much for remembering us."

"How are your son and daughter-in-law doing now?" I asked.

"It has been hard, but a year and a half after it happened, my daughter-in-law is just starting to do a little better," Miguel said with a quaver in his voice, but a proud smile on his face. "She is going to have a second child in a few months. A girl."

"May I offer you my happiest congratulations," I said kindly. "I know you're all looking forward to seeing that little one

when she arrives."

"Thank you." He hesitated. "Mr. Malachi, can I ask you a question? Do you think our little grandson is with the Lord in heaven?"

I put my hand on his shoulder. "Miguel, he was only three. An innocent baby. I'm sure he is waiting for you and the rest of his family in paradise."

"But, Mr. Malachi, our son and daughter-in-law, his parents, never had him baptized," Maria said anxiously.

I gave her a comforting smile. "It's alright, Maria. God never asked or said that babies or young children needed to be baptized. At that age they still don't know right from wrong. They are too young and they are innocent. All people are born without sin, and only when they come of age where they understand right from wrong, about God, and sin in their lives, does God then require that they repent and be baptized into Him. Your precious little grandson is safe in God's eyes."

The two of them couldn't speak for several long seconds as they held onto each other. I waited patiently until Miguel lifted his head and addressed me again.

"Mr. Malachi, my wife and I heard some news we wanted to ask you about," he said, pulling out a handkerchief to blow his nose. "We went over to the company about a week ago and learned from Jim Wilson that you had sold your business to some of the employees."

"That is true, I did."

"He also told us about your situation," Miguel added, eyeing me curiously, but with sympathy in his voice. "How are you doing?"

I gave him a reassuring smile. "Thanks for asking, Miguel, but I'm doing fine so far. There's no point in grieving about anything just yet."

"Mr. Malachi," Maria's voice was just a faint wisp. "Do you think you will see him soon, where you're going? Our little grandson?"

Something swept through me and shook me to the core.

Reality is a cold reminder. “I am sure I will see him soon, Maria.”

She crept closer to me, her eyes full of begging. “Will you give him a message for us, oh please, will you? That we and his parents love and miss him so very much?”

I stood very still, looking at the ground. Then I looked up at the pair of them waiting with bated breath for my response. Feeling suddenly weary, I held out my hand and Miguel slowly reached out and shook it. I then gave Maria one more light hug before stepping back again.

“I don’t know if I will be able to do as you ask,” I said softly. “But if I can deliver your message to your grandson, I will do my best to do just that.”

They needed no words to express how thankful they were. The expressions on their faces were enough to instill a quiet joy in my heart as we parted to go our separate ways. It uplifted me as I was reminded that not all stories of death had an unhappy ending.

Since it is a righteous thing with God to repay with tribulation those who trouble you, and to give you who are troubled rest with us when the Lord Jesus is revealed from heaven with His mighty angels, in flaming fire taking vengeance on those who do not know God, and on those who do not obey the gospel of our Lord Jesus Christ. -II Thessalonians 1:6-8

The days were quickly growing colder, and the air held a brisk snap in it that made one want to hide their face from any sudden gust of wind. About a week after my encounter with the woman at the gas station, I received a phone call during my morning coffee.

"Is this Malachi Winstead?"

I tried to place the voice as I politely answered in the affirmative, but I didn't recognize it at all. I could only tell that it was a young man.

"Oh, wonderful! I'm so glad I found you!" he exclaimed, his voice rising in sudden emotion that caused me to raise my eyebrows on my end of the line. *Who is this?*

"Ah...may I ask who is calling?"

"My name is Samuel Rodriguez. I believe you knew my father, Carlos Rodriguez."

That name immediately clicked in my head and I straightened up at once.

"Carlos? Yeah...wow," I rubbed the back of my neck, a slow grin spreading over my face. "It's been a really long time, but yes. I do know your father, young man. Known him for years."

"Yes sir, and that's why I'm asking to come meet with you."

"You want to meet with me?"

"Yes. I have many questions to ask you about my father. I know you two were close, and I think you might be able to help me find the answers I've been looking for. Would it be possible for us to meet?"

Carlos. I hadn't heard that name for quite some time. Just speaking to the man on the phone who claimed to be the son of my old friend filled my mind with memories. I realized that I wanted to meet the son. After all, I didn't have much time left. What could it hurt?

The following day I was on my way out of Portland, heading west toward the coast. The day was overcast, clouded and iron-gray. I hadn't seen the sun for at least three weeks, but that didn't bother me. I always loved the fall, and cloudy weather was a natural part of it. But Vicki didn't like it. She had never liked those hazy days with the weak light. She was always relieved when the sun came out again. She loved the sun. She was my own sun.

As I exited a tunnel, my thoughts twisted and turned with each bend in the road. I pulled out my cell phone, pressed a speed dial number, turned on the speakerphone, and sat it on the dashboard.

"Hey, Dad," Garrett answered on the second ring.

"Hi, son. How are you?"

"I'm fine. Are you ok? You having any problems?"

"No, no, I'm alright, son. Listen, I just wanted to let you know I'm on my way to the coast. So just in case something comes up, you know where I am."

"The coast? What's happening down there?"

"Nothing huge, but I'm going to be gone a couple of days. I'll ask your Uncle Dave to go by the house and collect the mail and such." I flexed my fingers around the steering wheel.

"Dad, I can take care of that for you."

"Well, maybe I'll have you call your uncle and let him know where I am," I teased.

For a moment there was silence on his end, then Garrett said quietly, "Dad, do you need company down there? Mary and I can come down tomorrow and stay with you."

My heart warmed at my son's generosity.

"No, son, I need some time on my own. It'll give me some time to think about things and pray. I'll be back in three or four days. Besides, I'm supposed to meet somebody there."

"Oh really?" Curiosity jumped back into his voice. "Who?"

"The son of an old military friend. He's in the Marines, and wanted to come meet with me. I thought I could use a day or two to myself down along the beach as well, so I just booked up the rest of the week down there."

"Ok, Dad. But just let us know if there's anything we can do. Oh, also, have you heard anything from the hospital?"

I gazed out the window toward the distant horizon. A sigh escaped my lips.

"No, I don't expect to hear from them before the fifteenth."

The ominous number hung heavily in the air, and I could tell Garrett was feeling the same way about the lack of news.

"Well Dad, you drive carefully," he told me soberly. "And call…Darrin! That's the third time your mother's called you!" His voice grew louder but suddenly faded as if he had muffled the phone to speak to another person. I smiled. Darrin was Garrett and Mary's only son and at the perfect age for extreme inquisitiveness and high maintenance energy.

I waited until Garrett finished speaking to his son before bringing the phone back to his ear again.

"Sorry, Dad. Was I ever, at that age –?"

"Of course you were," I laughed. He did, too.

"Well, like I was saying before, call us every day so we know you're ok. Not to sound like a nurse or anything, but..."

"I know, son. And I will. You take care and give Mary and the kids a hug from me, alright?"

"You got it, Dad. Take care of yourself."

I settled back against the car seat and smiled. It always uplifted me when I heard from my kids and their kids. I felt immeasurably blessed as I cruised down the highway with the ocean on my horizon and Andy Williams crooning through the radio speakers. I was glad I decided to book a couple of extra days at the beach house ahead of the time for my scheduled visitor. I needed the solitude. Or rather, the single companionship between a man and his Maker.

Two days later, I was strolling slowly along the Oregon beach, listening to the quiet music of the ocean waves, feeling the wet sand under my shoes and tasting the salt spray in the air. Gulls cried out overhead and a light mist fell. The water sparkled blue and burst in white foam against the rocks jutting up above the waves. Behind me, green cliffs rose into the sky that wrapped around and melted down toward the sand. Everything felt and smelled fresh and new. There's nothing like a long, early morning walk along the coast, and I took full advantage of it.

I walked a couple of miles south beside the water, then checked my watch. It wouldn't be long now before my visitor arrived at the beach house I had rented. I better head back. I paused along the way to turn over a piece of soaked driftwood and scoop up a couple of sea shells.

It was then that I saw it, half-buried in the sand. I don't know why my eyes were drawn to it, but I stopped and my fingers curled around it, lifting it up and shaking off the excess grains. It was a perfect sand dollar.

I looked at it in its round flawlessness without a single chip or crack, turning it over and over in my hand. I knew why my gaze had been directed toward it. It was like the sand dollar had been placed there for me to find. A perfect shell, simplistic in look but no less remarkable because of its commonplace color. In all the chaos and craze of this world, this sand dollar in my hand was like a quiet reminder that there was still beauty left and still joy to absorb from the little things in life. I rested the shell in the palm of my hand. A sudden tightness filled my chest, and I looked out over the water.

Oh Vicki...I know how much you always wanted to find a perfect sand dollar when we went to the beach. Now I have...and I can't give it to you.

An alarm on my watch beeped, and I reluctantly turned to continue my slow walk back to the beach house. I put the sand dollar safely in my pocket. Carrying it was almost like having a piece of her with me. The thought of her smiling with joy over such a find eased some of the heaviness in my heart as I drank in the ocean air and view.

I'm always with you, Malachi. You just won't always be able to see me. I might just be over the next horizon, she had once told me. I stared out over the waves as I walked, one hand in my pocket protecting the sand dollar. The distant line where the sky met the water filled me with a strange longing. I could almost believe Vicki was there, just beyond my sight, sailing away on a ship bound for somewhere I couldn't go just yet.

But not for long.

I looked up as I neared the beach house and saw someone standing on the upper deck, leaning on the railing and gazing out over the ocean. Upon walking closer I saw it was a Latino man in uniform. He evidently spotted me for he straightened up and raised one arm. My visitor had arrived. I waved back and hustled a little faster up the small rise on the beach, through the tall reeds and up the stairs to the top deck.

"Hello! You must be Carlos' son," I said, panting slightly from my energetic climb up the stairs.

"Yes sir, I am Samuel Rodriguez," the young man answered in a strong voice, shaking my hand with solemn respect. I looked him over. He was tall, well built, and good looking with dark eyes and hair. He stood very straight, with his shoulders back, and had almost snapped to attention when I addressed him. He wore a fitted Marine uniform. A handful of medals were already fastened on his chest. I raised my eyebrow when I saw them, impressed.

"Looks like you've seen some action."

"Yes sir, I'm home from my fourth deployment."

"Do you have a family?"

"A wife and three sons, sir."

I smiled with approval. "How about some coffee, Samuel? And won't you come and sit down?"

He nodded briefly, and I ushered him to one of the deck chairs. He sat with as good a posture as he stood. I hurried into the house, hooked two mugs over my thumb, and grabbed the full pot of coffee I had left to brew during my walk that was now ready.

"You'll have to pardon my being late," I said as I arranged

my offering on the small table between our chairs. Just a few hundred yards away, the sea hummed to itself as well as to us. "I was enjoying a particularly lovely walk along the beach this morning and lost track of the time." I shrugged and chuckled, hoping to get my visitor to relax a little. I understood his stiffness and ramrod formality were part of his career, but out here that didn't matter to me.

His black eyes followed the rich stream of coffee as it poured into the mugs, sending up a cloud of steam. Then his eyes met mine. "A fine stroll is a luxury," he remarked, and I felt relieved when a small smile lit up his face. We each picked up our coffee and sat back in our chairs.

"So, Samuel," I began, blowing on my coffee to cool it. "Just what is this visit about? How can I help you?"

"Like I said over the phone, Mr. Winstead, I believe you were close to my father, Carlos."

I balanced my coffee cup on my knee, my fingers barely closed around it to keep it from falling while protecting my skin from the hot china. "Please, just Malachi. Yes, we became friends a long time ago, your father and I. But I haven't seen him in over... whew, what is it...twenty-five, maybe thirty years." I shook my head, marveling at the realization.

He nodded soberly. He set his cup down and turned to face me.

"I am sorry to have to tell you that my father died in a plane crash when I was only two years old."

The news saddened me. Another thread cut, another friend gone.

"My mother died only a few years later of pneumonia," the young Marine went on after giving me a moment of respectful silence. "My grandmother raised my siblings and me. But, Malachi, before my mother died, she wrote a letter. And in that letter, she said that if I ever wanted to know the truth about my father's life that I should find a retired Navy SEAL by the name of Malachi Winstead."

He had pulled out the mentioned letter, well creased as if it had been well read and had traveled many miles in his pocket. He looked back up at me from reading the line which bore my own name in confirmation that I was indeed the one sitting before him.

"Before I joined the military, when I was about eighteen, I searched for you several times but could never find any strong leads as to where you were. After becoming a Marine and getting deployed, I suppose over the years I sort of gave up on the idea of ever finding you. Then about a year ago, I was on duty with an intelligence officer. We became friends, and one day I happened to mention to him that I had been looking for somebody in the Navy but couldn't find him. He told me he could find anyone who had been in the military, even a retired Navy SEAL, and said he would see what he could do to help me.

Then just a few weeks ago, on my way home from my deployment, I got a phone call from him."

"I guess he found me, since you're here," I remarked with a wide smile.

Samuel raised an eyebrow. "He said you were harder to track down than most, but he gave me your phone number, which was how I was able to contact you a few days ago. He also told me that, if I needed to see you, I better do it soon." He gave me a look of curiosity. I raised one shoulder, attempting to keep the current conversation thread light.

"So now here I am, Malachi. That's why I called to ask if you would meet with me. Please, sir. I need to know about my father and what kind of man he was."

His earnestness intrigued me. What young man in his right mind wouldn't want to delve into the past of his father and see what kind of example he could follow from him? However, I hesitated. A world of recollections sat on the tip of my tongue, but would they be what Samuel wanted to hear? Would he walk away today with any regrets over what I had to tell him?

I looked back at him steadily, then said, "Are you sure you want to know everything I can tell you about your father?"

He straightened up once more, every inch the professional Marine that he was. "Yes sir. Good or bad, I need to know the truth about my father."

My eye caught the glint of the medals on his uniform. *You've earned the right to know*, I thought, and heaved a deep sigh.

"You're asking me to tell you about a part of your dad's life that ties to my own. It's a part of my life that I don't talk about. I've spent the last thirty years of my life trying to forget about that piece of my past."

Samuel didn't press me. He sat very still and waited. I knew he wasn't going anywhere until he got the answers he so keenly sought. I would have to relive those days that haunted the darkest corners of my memory. What was worse, those memories involved Samuel's father.

But he has the right to know. I stood up and began pacing across the deck, searching for a place to begin.

"Your dad and I were the best of friends for over thirty years," I started, placing my hands on the railing and looking out to sea. "Your dad was a man's man. You could always trust his word. He was fearless. He never gave up on anything he wanted. He had this optimism that remained strong no matter the situation."

I turned to face him, and Samuel's face was lit up as he hung on my every word. I could tell he was genuinely intrigued.

"Time passed, and we became stronger than friends. When we entered the Navy, we were brothers in arms. We lived a life of danger and adventure. We lived on the edge so much that it became a part of us, and balancing between life and death was a part of our everyday lives. He had my back and I had his. I believe either one of us would've taken a bullet for the other had it been necessary."

Talking about those far-off days and standing there breathing in the ocean air brought the past back to life so vividly for me that I was amazed by just how much I could remember that I had tried so hard to forget. I continued to walk the deck as I told my story, and Samuel remained very still in his seat, watching my every move.

"Our first encounter took place after we had gone through

boot camp in San Diego. Both your father and I had enlisted to be Navy SEALs, and after boot camp we found ourselves at the Navy SEAL Training Center in southern California. The first time I saw your dad, we were standing in a roll call line of about thirty men who were there for the new class. The captain was telling us how only a few of us, maybe five or six at most, would survive the course and become SEALs. Your dad was standing next to me. The first words he said to me were, "I'm going to be one of those few. I'm going to be the best they've ever seen."

"Well, I thought for a few seconds about what he just said, then I said..."

Samuel leaned forward. "What did you say?"

I stared down at my hands. "I said...'Are you kidding me? No wet-back Mexican is going to show me up because I'll be number one in this class.'"

Samuel let out a long, low whistle. I wasn't proud of myself, but that's what had happened, and I was going to tell the truth.

"As the words left my mouth, he swung his duffel bag at me, and knocked me backward. Well, that caught our captain's attention before it could go any further, and before we knew it he was on top of us. 'So you boys want to fight instead of listen?' he said. 'How about you hit the deck and start giving me push-ups while I march the class down to the operations building. I'll be back for you later and when I do, you still better be doing push-ups.'"

"Sounds like the beginning of a wonderful friendship," the young marine said with a chuckle.

"Oh, throughout the entirety of our training, Carlos and I competed in everything. Neither one of us was going to let the other outdo him. But by the time we had finished, we considered each other the best of friends. Our superior officers noted our competition, but allowed it to continue because it gave us the ability to give our all and do our best. They vamped up our missions and made training as challenging as possible without being impossible. We were undefeated. There wasn't a two-man team better than your dad and me, and soon everybody knew it. As the others fell out by ones and twos, we stayed on. And from there we went through jump school, sniper school, and basic flight training. When we were finished, I guess you could say we thought of ourselves as a couple of real killing machines."

I refilled our coffee cups and tried to gauge Samuel's reaction to my story. So far, he seemed pleased by what he heard. I sat back down and bounced my knee slowly up and down as I tried to decide where to take the narrative next.

"Shortly after training ended, the government began a top-secret missions group, and because of our extreme prowess, Carlos and I were selected. I don't believe that to this day it is known that there were four two-man teams to carry out these missions."

"Isn't that classified information?" he interrupted. "Should you be telling me this?"

I shook my head. "The operation was discontinued not long after I retired. I suppose it's archived back in the annals of government secrets now for future generations to discover. But anyway, Carlos and I were a team. Occasionally we worked with the others, but mostly we worked by ourselves. The whole time we were SEALs, your dad and I were used by a top-secret organization. Within the first six years, we were the only team left of the original four. New teams were formed, but they would always give your dad and me the most difficult jobs. If anywhere in the world a town, village, or government was being terrorized by corrupt leaders trying to take over, we were the ones contacted and sent to take out the troublemakers."

"Take them out. You mean kill them."

"It was some of the most hazardous work in the world. With Carlos and me, it never seemed to bother us. We were taking out bad people. It never occurred to us to really think about the eternal consequences of what we were doing. And some of them were the worst trash you can imagine..." I paused, surprised by the harshness in my voice. Taking a deep breath, I went on. "After twenty years of service, we could retire. So we did."

Samuel pursed his lips. "Was my dad ever wounded?" he

asked.

"You can't do that kind of work and walk away clean every time. Your dad and I were both shot more than once, but fortunately it was never fatal. Our job came along with unforeseen parasites, broken bones, strange illnesses picked up in foreign countries, and so forth."

Samuel grimaced, but nodded thoughtfully.

"There were no purple hearts given either," I added. "Because, officially, we didn't exist, nor our work either. We had a lot of close calls, but providence kept us from dying in some remote jungle or desert at the hands of some really bad people."

I looked down to pour some more coffee and saw the hands on my watch pointing to noon.

"Hey, there's a great seafood place just a little ways down the beach. I ate there for dinner last night." I stood up. "You want to grab a bite?"

"Absolutely." Samuel stood up and followed me down the stairs. I suggested we walk along the beach a little ways back from the waterfront, since it was only a half mile or so to the restaurant. We strolled along slowly, taking deep breaths of the salty air and listening to the waves roll.

"My mother told me that my dad worked for the military after he got out of the Navy," Samuel remarked, glancing at me as though asking a question. I shook my head.

"No, not exactly. Carlos and I went our separate ways after retirement to settle down to civilian life, but that didn't take. So about a year or so later, we looked each other up. Neither one of us had found a job or career that really meant anything to us."

"So what happened?"

"Well, we thought it would be neat to start our own business together, but we needed a lot of money we didn't have, so we decided to put all of that expensive training and military experience we had to work for us." I shoved my hands deep into my pockets. I was getting to the part of the story I wish I could erase from my existence. "We had known about, or had had dealings with, many of the world's arms dealers, so we started a company delivering all kinds of weapons and military supplies to the dictators, war lords, and drug dealers we used to kill or take in."

Samuel didn't answer for a long time. I almost couldn't bring myself to look at him. It was as if I could feel his shock and disapproval boring through me.

"Those kinds of people," I said quietly, "the people we worked for and supplied, were the scum of the earth. We knew them as maggots, yet the most dangerous people you could do business with. You can't imagine how dangerous our work was. When we delivered to them, they had it in their minds to close the deals by keeping the arms and their money and just killing us. Usually in the worst way they could."

"How did you survive?" Samuel asked in a tone that made all the guilt and regret I had tried to suppress come back in a burning flood.

Just get through the rest of it as quickly as possible.

"It was simple," I said aloud. "Your dad and I just had to be smarter than they were, and we were. We always went into the operation believing we were going to keep the arms, the dealers' money, and kill all of them. It was high-paying work too, because you never knew for sure if you had a tomorrow coming. There's a big demand for arms around the world. We had one job after the other. Planning, delivering, and surviving. That's what our world consisted of."

Samuel stopped walking. I turned to look back at him, forcing myself to meet his eyes.

"Did you or Dad ever marry?"

The question was so pointed and unexpected that I answered without thought.

"No. There was never time for that, and we weren't interested in making widows. But..." I felt my chest tighten. "... There were women for, for comfort, and alcohol for pain."

I saw him flinch, and felt my own stomach turn over. Dredging up these recollections was starting to give me a headache. So much water had rolled under the bridge, yet time could never completely erase the resonance and understanding of what I had done as a younger man.

Samuel seemed hesitant to keep walking with me. I wondered if I had lost him. It was what I had been afraid of at the start, and said softly, "Samuel, you asked me to tell you the truth about your father and how I knew him. The fact that his life corresponds with mine is part of the story. Do you want me to go on?"

He fixed me with a sudden glare that froze my steps. "Yes. I want to know everything. Let's keep going."

He marched past me without another word, and I followed him on down the beach. We didn't say anything more to each other until we were seated at the open-air fish-and-chips place with our lunch in front of us. After eating in silence for a while, Samuel turned to me again.

"So, is there more to this story?" he asked.

I looked at him and his starched uniform, the badges of honor on his jacket. Taking one last bite, I wiped my hands on a napkin.

"I believe I've told you all that you need to know about your father. I hope I've satisfied your questions."

He stared at me. "Mr. Malachi, I think you haven't told me all of the story. Please, don't try to protect me. I really want to know."

"But, do you really *need* to know is what I'm asking."

He looked down at his lap, tapping his fingers on the table. Without looking at me, he said firmly, "Sir, I don't know if I need to know. But I'm asking you to tell me anyway."

When I didn't answer, he burst out, "I'm his son! I think I have a right to know!"

Once again I looked long and hard at the young man sitting across the table from me. He looked almost desperate, almost like a boy again. A boy who so badly wanted to know who his father was, the father he had never known, and would probably never know.

"Come with me," I said shortly, and throwing some money on the table, got up and began walking back toward the beach.

Samuel hurried after me.

"There were a number of jobs your dad and I did besides moving arms," I said as we walked back down to the sand. The sky was still hidden behind the clouds, even at midday. It cast a strange light on our faces. "Sometimes we took out one of the bad guys and sometimes we moved people from one country to another. People didn't really want to go through customs. But," and I stopped to emphasize my next words, "we never moved drugs. That I can promise you, Samuel."

I wasn't sure by the expression on his face if he completely believed me or not. What could I do but go on?

"Several years after we started this kind of work, three things happened that would change your dad and me from working together. Changed our lives forever, in fact."

I felt his pace quicken ever so slightly. "What happened?"

I sighed. "It was a simple job. We took a contract to bring two people from eastern Mexico across the border into Texas. What your dad and I didn't know was that these people were related to one of the Mexican drug lords who was financing the trip. Nor did we know that the CIA and Mexican Secret Police were planning to drop down on this drug lord and take him out. Maybe he knew that. But I don't know. Anyway, we set the plane down on a dark, dusty runway about fifty miles west of Cancun. There was a car there to meet us with a bag full of money and three people: a big guy and two kids in their early twenties who looked scared to death. We didn't know who they were, probably the drug lord's kids. We got the money and the passengers loaded and took off heading north across the Gulf of Mexico, but didn't know we were being followed by another plane. As we crossed the twelve-mile limit, a couple of F-18s showed up, one on either side of us, and told us to put the plane down at the Corpus Christi Naval Air Station and if we didn't, they would shoot us out of the sky."

Samuel's eyes were wide like truck headlights. "What did you do then?"

"Well, your dad and I both knew that if we landed that plane, there'd be no getting away. It would be ten to twenty in the federal penitentiary. We had barely a few minutes to do something. And your dad," I pointed my finger at Samuel. "Your dad just looked at me and said, 'Just do what I tell you.' And in that moment, as soon as he said that, I had this crazy feeling that we might get out of this alive and free of orange jumpsuits. Carlos jumped into the backseat of the plane between the two kids and put his arms around both of them. He told them, 'Don't worry, we'll get you down.' Then he told me, 'Drop the speed and fall back. The jets will have to do a one-eighty if they want to pull back around.' I pulled us back and your dad just banged the heads of those kids together and knocked them out. Then he shoved them out of the door with their luggage and the money. It was a dark night, and by the time the jets had relocated beside us, all of it was done and we were heading down for a final approach."

Samuel's mouth fell open. "What then?" he demanded.

"Once we landed, they couldn't find anything, so they couldn't hold us. They seemed to believe we were a decoy."

"Wow," he exclaimed. "That's incredible. I can't believe you weren't shot!"

I shuffled my feet in the sand, watching it crumble against my shoes. "Your dad and I had killed a lot of people over the years, but they had always been bad people that we thought of as sending on their way to hell. But this was the first time we shed innocent blood, that we knew of, to save our own lives. I never... it's not something you can come back from, no matter who you are. Your dad and I were never the same after that. Yes, we had escaped with our lives, but at what cost?" I rubbed my forehead wearily. Everything suddenly looked so bleak. Telling everything to this young man made me feel exposed and vulnerable in such a raw way. Those torturous secrets had been mine alone for almost half of my life.

And yet, it was freeing in a sense to unburden my past to another soul. Even if I was despised for it. And I knew I had been forgiven long ago by the One Who had given me the conscience which had pricked my heart. Many a sleepless night of prayers and tears had been spent in enduring the agony of a soul in desperate need of cleansing. I swallowed against the lump in my throat and tried to force my thoughts back to the here and now.

"We began to think about quitting. Neither one of us wanted to keep going with that kind of work after that last incident. We had already signed other contracts, but we knew which one would be the last."

I knew Samuel wanted to hear more, but I also knew he was disappointed by what I had already told him. *I didn't want to tell you in the first place, son.* But I had come too far to stop now. The least I could do for him was to go ahead and finish the story.

"The second thing that turned our world around happened a couple of months later on the job that your dad and I agreed would be our last. We had been offered a job with a big security company in Houston, Texas. We knew the owner and had worked with him a few times over the years. It was one of those high-dollar companies that protected people world-wide. We would start off by managing our own teams."

I sighed again. "We had been looking for some high-paying desk jobs in our spare time, and had promised each other months ago that this would be our last job in the field. But neither one of us knew how literally that really would be our last job."

"What do you mean?" Samuel didn't take his eyes off me.

I didn't look at him. "It was going to take three flights to get everything delivered. It was for a rebel army in Guatemala. We had been paid in advance because of the high risks. We were to collect the final payment upon delivery. Everything had gone according to plan, and as we lifted off the dirt runway there at the edge of the jungle, there in the trees...there must have been a whole army hiding."

Samuel caught his breath. "An army?"

"They may have been government troops. They might even have been the ones we were delivering to who were hoping to get their money back. Whoever they were, they were intent on shooting us down." My voice faded as the sound of remembered gunfire exploded from a forest of trees and passed through my hearing. Only a memory, but as real to me as the sand and water on this beach.

"Within seconds, there were thousands of rounds going right through our plane. The wings were hit. The engine was hit, and started to fail." I stopped and cocked my head. "You know," I mused, "I remember seeing hundreds of tiny beams of light shining all around me in that plane, in all the chaos, where the bullet holes were. It's funny how the mind holds onto those insignificant details."

"But you didn't crash?"

"To this day, I cannot explain why we didn't crash; why both your dad and I weren't dead by the end of it all. For some reason, God intended us to live. Somehow we stayed in the air and made it back to Phoenix where an airplane dealer friend of ours could help us out. He agreed to buy our planes when we told him we were quitting the business, and when the deal was done, Carlos flew out that very night to meet with our security company's office in Washington D.C. I was to go down to the office in Houston. We met up in a hotel bar in Phoenix before our flights. Somehow, I think he and I both knew, without saying anything, that for the first time in many years we were about to go our separate ways for good.

"Well, Mal," he told me, raising his glass, "It's been crazy. Here's to the end of it."

"And here's to the beginning of something hopefully better," I told him. We walked out to the street where he flagged a cab. As he opened the door to get in, he turned back and grabbed my hand. He didn't say anything, he just shook my hand and looked me in the eye like he was about to tell me something. Thirty years of friendship, teamwork, and countless adventures and dangers coming to an end were summed up in that one moment of unspoken farewell. Then he was gone. And I never saw him again."

I could see the beach house in sight now. I stopped on the sand and Samuel stopped a few paces behind me.

"Samuel, your dad was my best friend. He was always a hero in my book. Even though we didn't meet in person, we did talk a few times on the phone. I heard that he had finally met and married your mother while he was stationed in London."

"But how was it that you never saw my dad again?" Samuel asked.

"Remember I said there were three things that changed our lives forever," I answered. "The loss of our passengers over the gulf, the shot-up plane that never should have gotten us home, and then the third thing...which happened only to me."

"Which was?" He was turning back into the authoritative Marine again. I took a few steps away from him down toward the water. The ocean raced up the wet sand, just curling against the tips of my shoes. With my back to the young man, I braced myself to continue.

"I never went to work for that security company. Though I made it to Houston, I didn't go to the office. Something happened that changed everything."

I turned around, my hands in my pockets, and saw Samuel looking at me curiously. I knew the question spinning through his mind and couldn't help but smile.

"The day after your dad left, I scheduled a flight to Houston. Before I left, I went back to collect any personal items that might have been left on the planes we had just sold. While I was looking around, the head mechanic, Ira, who had been in charge of maintenance on our planes for years came over to me. He said, 'Mr. Winstead, I have personally counted the holes in this plane, and there are more than a thousand. The engine is bust. How the two of you did not die or that this plane remained in the air as long as it did I don't know. You must be the two luckiest guys in the world.' I just stopped and looked at him. I said, 'I don't understand it either. But we lived.' And then just saying that out loud caused something to hit me like a bolt of lightning. I was alive. And I should have been dead, but I wasn't."

I brushed my fingers against the sand dollar in my pocket, and slowly pulled it out. I should have been killed. But God spared me. Why?

"Is that the end of the story?" Samuel questioned, pulling back my thoughts. By this time, we were climbing back up the stairs to the top deck of the beach house. We found our original chairs and sat down to rest.

I glanced down at the shell in my hand and rubbed it between my fingers before sliding it back into my pocket. "Not quite. The mechanic then said to me, 'Did you ever stop and think what would've happened to you if you had died on this plane?' I said I guess I just would've been dead. I had grown so used to the near presence of death everyday that the thought of it didn't really affect me. Ira told me, 'A man once said that life is the childhood of immortality. We will all live forever some place when this life is over. The question is where?' And you know Samuel," I said earnestly, "as I listened to this mechanic, all I could think about were the incidents of those innocent souls drowning because of us, and a plane full of holes that never should have come home. Then all the other things I had done to help wicked people around the world came to mind. And it got me thinking, if this Ira was right and there really was a life after death...then where would I be? And if I had a choice, what would my decision be? Something came over me that made me desperate for an answer to this question. And it was then Ira said, 'Mr. Winstead, would you like to know what would have happened to you if you had gone down with this plane?' I said sure, and he just said, 'Let's get together this evening after I'm off work and I can discuss it with you.'"

"Well I wanted an answer right then, and said I couldn't make it that night because my flight to Houston left in less than an hour. So he said, 'Ok, but wait just a minute and let me get something for you.' And he ran off to his office and came back with a DVD in a cardboard sleeve. 'Please, just take a look at this,' he said to me when he put it in my hand. 'I'm sure it will give you the answer you're looking for.'"

"I looked at the DVD face and the title on it was something about where do you go when you die. That seemed reasonable, so I stuck it in my bag and thanked him, and promised I'd take a look at it. And as the 707 flight lifted off, I got out my laptop to check my travel instructions for when I landed in Houston. When I pulled out my laptop, there was the DVD next to it. I looked at it, and remembered my promise, so I put it in my laptop, thinking maybe I would watch a few minutes of it. By the time my plane landed, I had watched the entire DVD. I learned things I never imagined I could know. In just those few short hours, I was able to understand what had been hazy confusion before."

Samuel looked at me like he himself was confused. "So you got religion, or...?"

"I wouldn't say I 'got' religion. What I would say is that I learned the truth that I had never known before. And learning that sparked a desire in me to study even further about this sensational news. I called up Ira with more questions after watching the DVD, and he told me to call again when I got to my hotel. So, when I reached my room, I did. About an hour later, there was a knock on my door."

"Ira came all the way down to Houston in only an hour? That's impossible!"

I smiled. "It wasn't Ira."

"Then who was it?"

"A tall, lanky fella I had never seen before in my life who promptly stuck out his hand and said, 'Hey there, I'm Kevin Coleman. I understand you have some questions that need answering.'

'Uh...yeah, I guess I do,' I answered cautiously, not knowing what I was getting into or how this stranger even knew who I was or what I wanted to know.

He wasn't even fazed. He just held up a Bible and said, 'Ira Banks contacted me. I'm a friend of his, and I live here in Houston. I have the answer here to all of your questions, Mr. Winstead.'

And with that, he just pushed his way into the room and, after a few more minutes of introduction, I felt at ease enough to start asking the many questions on my mind. Kevin opened his Bible and showed me the answers to all of them. We sat there in my hotel room til early morning, only taking a break to order pizza for dinner. It was 2 A.M. when we decided to rest for the night and pick back up the following afternoon. And that was the beginning of the end of my old life, Samuel. Even when I was overwhelmed by the overload of all this new information I was receiving, I knew for certain that I was moving on to greater things. And my life was never the same again."

Samuel sat very still with his hands clasped between his knees, his strong shoulders hunched forward. His brow was twisted in deep thought.

"Do you think..." he faltered, "do you think my dad ever found what you found? That he changed his life before he died?"

I leaned back and folded my arms, uncertain what to say. I hoped my old friend had found the truth, but I also had no way of knowing now if he had.

"Samuel, I don't know if your father obeyed what is written in the Bible. But I do know that your father was a smart man. If he knew there was truth out there that would help him be the best man he could be, he would go after it with all his might. Believe me, nothing could stop him."

Samuel looked at me, and I saw the eyes of a little boy again in a man's face. Once again I felt the hollow ache of cold comfort.

Then Samuel rose fluidly from his seat. He held out his hand. I stood up too, and as I shook his hand I remembered doing the same to his father so many years ago.

"Thank you, Malachi," he told me, his voice wavering just a little. "You have given me something invaluable today, and I will be forever grateful to you."

"What is that, Samuel?"

He gave me a small smile. "The truth about my father. Now I feel as if I know the person he was."

"But is the knowing better than the not knowing?" I asked. "You know the truth now, but there was plenty of it that I know I'm not proud of and wish I could say were only stories and not what really happened. I don't want you to spend the rest of your life being disappointed in your father. Remember him for changing his heart."

He looked at me steadily. "Knowing is better. Knowing will help me be a better man for my wife and children. Knowing will make me stronger in my determination to do what is right."

"I pray you always will, Samuel," I said soberly. "I pray you always will."

He nodded once and saluted me before turning on his heel. He reached the stairs and turned back. I was struck by how much he looked like his father, but even more so by his last words to me.

"Don't dwell on your past, Malachi," he said. "If you're the man I think you are based on what you've told me today, there must still be a plan for you. It's the looking ahead that gets us where we need to go, not looking back."

But I say to you that whoever divorces his wife for any reason except sexual immorality causes her to commit adultery; and whoever marries a woman who is divorced commits adultery. -Matthew 5:32

Chapter 6

The Lawyer

My conversation with Samuel Rodriguez was still rolling over my thoughts a couple of days after I returned from the coast, when I received a phone call from my lawyer, Cason Edwards.

"Hey, Malachi. Do you want to come by my office about noon tomorrow to sign the last of the legal documents regarding the will?"

"Sure. Then we could have lunch afterward."

"Ok, then. Let's say eleven, alright?"

"Sounds good," I replied.

The following day, I drove to the office to meet with him. After he shook my hand and placed the necessary documents in front of me, I was again struck by a deep sense of reality. This was my will lying on the table before my eyes. The entailment of my executive estate. Seeing my signature on the bottom line was so surreal in light of the circumstances.

"Malachi, your signing these will finish off the rest of the paperwork," Cason told me. "Everything else will be taken care of just as you instructed."

I dragged my fountain pen across the smooth white paper, dotting the last i with careful precision.

"I want to thank you for all your help, Cason," I said, clicking the cap back on my pen and replacing it in my coat pocket. "This means a lot to me."

"You know I'm glad to be of help to you and make sure everything is in order." He stood up, straightening his tie. "Now, how about some lunch?"

I stood up, eager to get out of the office. "Absolutely. What did you have in mind?"

Cason grinned and held out his hand, gesturing for me to walk out first. "I know a great place within walking distance if you're up for a steak."

"That sounds good to me," I agreed.

We arrived at the restaurant, and as we found a corner table and picked up our menus, I noticed Cason seemed a little fidgety, as if he wasn't sure exactly what to do with himself. He rested his chin on one hand, then the other, moved the condiments around on the table top, kept fiddling with his shirt cuffs, and so forth. I watched him from the corner of my eye, but didn't say anything until after the waiter brought us our meal. When Cason picked up his fork and turned it in his hand for a few seconds, I asked him outright if anything was wrong.

He looked up as if I had surprised him, then he chuckled in a half-hearted way and rubbed the side of his neck.

"Ah, sorry, I don't mean to be..." he stopped, then said suddenly, "Can I tell you a story, Malachi?"

I put down my glass of ice tea. "Well, sure, Cason. You look like you've got something on your mind."

"Because I think maybe you could help me with something," he said, twisting the fork into his pile of mashed potatoes.

"Well, I'll see what I can do."

He looked around as though to make sure nobody was watching him, causing me to do the same, wondering what could possibly make him afraid of anybody overhearing our conversation. Then he scooted his chair closer to the table, leaning in to speak to me across our sizzling steaks.

"Malachi," he began, "I know you're a member of the Lord's church."

"Yes, I am," I answered, taking a bite of meat.

"Many years ago, my wife Cindy and I were also members of the Lord's church in Denver. Cindy was raised in the church, but I wasn't a member until about six months before our marriage."

I nodded with understanding.

"Maybe it was my hope of marrying her that had moved me along, I don't know," Cason murmured, tracing the rim of his glass and rubbing the condensation between his fingers. "She was very much in love with me. But she was also a very moral Christian woman, so there wasn't going to be any, well, messing around in our relationship before we were married. I guess that was something I had never really experienced with anyone before. I was one of those kinds of guys who..." He hesitated, and I put down my fork. "What, Cason?"

He sighed. "I was the type of guy who had been with a lot of women. And, after we were married a few years, I began to miss that lifestyle."

I knew where his story was going, and judging from his uncomfortable, restless manner, I also knew he didn't want to tell me. He shook his head a few times and rubbed his chin.

"You know, I guess...I guess I simply missed the excitement. I knew I had never really been in love with Cindy, and when I was with her I felt like I couldn't have what I really wanted. So by the time our fifth anniversary came up, I had committed adultery a number of times."

"Oh, Cason."

"I felt that, in fairness to my wife, our marriage needed to end. So I told her what I had done," Cason said stoutly. His face was hard but his voice revealed otherwise. "She was heartbroken, of course. I thought that would be the end of it, and I would be free. But Cindy said no, she would forgive me and do her best to fulfill all my needs and desires. She didn't want to divorce. I couldn't believe it, you know?" He viciously rubbed the back of his neck as if it pained him. He brought his hand down on the table and stared at his untouched food. "After four more years and two kids, I knew our marriage wasn't working for me. But I knew if I just outright divorced her she couldn't remarry and be right with her God, and I didn't want her to pay for my choices."

Cason looked me straight in the eyes; his were full of emotion.

"I truly believed she deserved a husband who would be

faithful to her," he said pleadingly. "So I called up a friend of mine and told her I needed a favor." Cason tossed his hand and smiled bitterly. "After we spent a weekend away together, I went back to Cindy and told her what I had done. But she said she wanted us to work it out. She said God hates divorce." He pressed his lips together and stared out the window. "She begged me to go see a marriage counselor with her, to get some help. But after a couple of weeks it finally got through to her that it wouldn't work. So I moved out. I left for California, and I left the church."

Cason leaned his head in his hands. I folded mine beside my plate and waited.

"Three years ago," he mumbled through his fingers, "she came down with lung cancer." He dragged his hands down and away from his face, gazing upward. "It was fatal. When I heard, I went to see her. But it was too late. I went to her funeral, but all I could think of was how I had wrecked her life. She had always been a good wife, a good mother, and a good Christian. So I knew she would go to Heaven." He played with the edge of his napkin. "The place I believe you're going, Malachi."

I leaned toward him, having an idea of what was coming. "Is there something I can do to help you, Cason?" I asked gently.

"Could you give her a message for me?" he burst out. "Just tell her to please forgive me for what I did to her. I don't deserve forgiveness, but I want her to know I'm sorry I hurt her so much."

"I don't know, Cason. I don't know if I can do that. But if I can, I will."

He nodded rapidly, looking anywhere but my face. I ran my tongue across my lower lip, trying to find the right words to say. I knew it had been hard for him telling me all this.

"Cason, you know it's not too late."

"Too late," he scoffed. "I think it is."

"I'm talking about you, Cason," I said earnestly. "Jesus died so that you could be forgiven of those sins you've just confessed to me. All it takes is for you to repent of all your sins, and God is faithful to forgive. You can be with your Cindy in paradise someday."

Cason took a deep breath. "You're probably right, Malachi. But I've been living this way so long...and I've lost the desire and the will to give it up."

"But you can do it!" I exclaimed. I looked around at the families dining around us and quickly lowered my voice. "I know that God will help you if you try. Wanting to do right is half the battle. With God's help, you can find the will to get out of sin! And I know people in the church will help you. I'll help you!"

He sat still for a moment, then picked up his silverware and began sawing on his steak. "What you're saying makes sense." He took a bite and rubbed the tip of his nose briefly with the back of his knuckles. "Maybe someday, I'll take your advice."

I understood our conversation was over and sadly returned my attention to my cooled meal.

Here is one so lost, he has lost all hope.

"Hey, thanks for listening," Cason told me when we parted company after eating. "Please try to give Cindy my message."

I grasped his hand. "I can't promise anything, but if I'm allowed, I will. And you, please, seek the Lord. He will give you the help you need."

The lawyer broke my handshake and took a step back. "Like I said. Maybe I will."

Whataburger was my favorite fast-food stop, so I would often grab a bite to eat there on my way home from work, back when I was still CEO of the company. Now that I was officially retired, I had to drive more out of my way to get to Whataburger, but it was always worth it, and the burgers I had there would never disappoint.

Having spent the day in town after finishing up with legal matters, I decided to have a cheeseburger for dinner. When I went inside and placed my order, I sat down in a booth and folded my arms on the table, gazing out the window. Then my phone vibrated. I pulled it out and saw a message from my granddaughter, bringing an instant smile to my face.

Hey, Grandpa! I was thinking about you today. School is

great, but I miss seeing you all the time. Love you so much! P.S. All my friends like the car.

I chuckled. Just as I placed the phone back in my pocket, a woman suddenly popped out of nowhere and stood at my elbow.

"Aren't you Malachi Winstead?"

"Yes, ma'am, that's my name. You have me at a disadvantage though. May I ask who you are?"

"Amy Thompson." She reached over to shake my hand, and I noticed she wore a long fur coat and satin wrist gloves, an odd choice of accessories for a fast-food joint. "I believe you knew my dad, Bert Morgan."

Lately I seemed to know everybody's parents or distant relatives. "Ah...let me see, Bert Morgan..." I stretched my arms out on either side of my edge of the table. "If I remember correctly, did he live over on East 5th and work at the university?"

She smiled, evidently pleased. Tucking a strand of her long blond hair behind her ear, she cupped her hands around the clasp wallet she held. "That's true! You came over a couple of times to study the Bible with him. But that was years ago. You probably don't remember it."

"No," I said slowly, holding up one hand. The memory, though fuzzy, was starting to come back to me. "I think I remember now. That must have been..." I stopped and whistled. "Four or five years ago at least, my goodness. How is your dad doing?"

She arched her neck and gazed off to the side. "He went on to heaven a little over a year ago."

"I'm very sorry to hear of your loss," I told her. "I always found your dad to be a good-hearted man. I remember how he loved to read the Bible."

A server walked over and set down a tray with my dinner on it. Awkwardly I slid the tray a few inches toward myself, then looked up at the lady, who didn't seem to be going away.

"Won't you, uh, join me?" I offered, gesturing to the empty seat across from me.

She smiled pleasantly, and slid into the other side of the booth. "Oh, thank you. I was hoping I would find you, Mr. Winstead."

"Malachi, please." I started to unwrap my cheeseburger.

"Malachi, then. I've wanted to tell you something my dad said. Before he passed away, that is."

"Sure. You don't mind if I..." I held up the burger, and she quickly waved her gloved hands and shook her head. "Oh, please, go right ahead. I can't stay long anyway and I don't want to interrupt your meal."

"You're no trouble," I assured her politely. "But can you give me a minute while I say a prayer?"

She nodded, and when I looked up a few short moments later she was toying with her gloves and staring out the window.

"So," I said, and she started. "What did you want to tell me, something about your father?"

She cleared her throat and straightened the fur around her shoulders. "Yes, Malachi. See, my father always said that you were a man of the book, and if he had any kind of question, I mean about the Bible, that you would be the man he would call on first."

"Well, that was kind of him," I remarked, sliding aside the ketchup containers with only a slight grimace on my face. Condiments on French fries simply ruined the taste for me. My grandkids had been trying to get me to like ketchup and mustard for years now, but I steadfastly refused.

"My dad told me that after your visits with him that he thought you were a good man, and that you knew and stood by the Bible and the truth," Amy Thompson went on, now fiddling with the strand of pearls around her neck. "But after awhile, you stopped coming by. Every so often, he would tell me how great it would be if he could find you and talk with you again about some questions he had. But we didn't know how to find you."

She looked at me piercingly, and I slowed my eating as what she said sank in.

"That's too bad, Mrs. Thompson. Had I known he wanted me, I would've come by to see him."

She shook her hair back and rolled her lips together a couple of times. "Well, it doesn't matter now. A couple of years ago he came down with Alzheimer's. It was very fast. In just a few months, he didn't know who I was, or who my mom was. We never really got to talk again."

"I'm sorry to hear that," I repeated with a sigh. I knew how vicious and deteriorating that dreadful mind disease is.

Amy scooted up against the edge of her side of the table. "Can I ask you a question, Malachi? When you, when you get to heaven, will you tell my dad that I love him?" She squeezed her hands together. "And that I miss him very much."

"Mrs. Thompson–"

"Amy, please," she said gently.

"There's something I need to tell you, Amy."

"Alright, what is it?"

I pulled the straw in my Dr. Pepper up and down a few times. "When I studied the Bible with your dad, with Bert, he was always eager to learn but he never wanted to do all that God asked of him. He told me he would think about becoming a Christian someday, but as long as I knew him, he didn't obey the Gospel. Was he ever baptized, Amy?"

Her face was like a stone. She opened her mouth, but all that came out was a short, "Ah..."

"Amy," I said very soberly, "if your dad was never baptized into Christ, then as much as it hurts me to tell you, it won't be possible for me to give your dad a message from you. He won't be where I'm going."

"You're saying he won't be with you in heaven," she said in a flat voice. Before I could do more than nod once, she stood up abruptly. I could see she was hurt.

"My dad was a good man, Malachi. He read his Bible every day, and he loved his family." Her face was now turning red, and her voice caught on the ends of her words. "His funeral was held in a church, and the priest pardoned all his sins and said he would be with Jesus for eternity." She grew even angrier the longer she spoke. "How dare you say he won't be in heaven! Who are you to judge my father?"

Her voice was growing louder and louder. A few people were looking at us now. Embarrassed and sorrowful, I tried to calm the woman down, but she backed away from my peaceably outstretched hand.

"You are nothing but an evil old man who enjoys hurting others!" she raged. "You know something? You are right! You *won't* be where my father is!"

I leaned back from her accusing finger jabbing toward my face. Before I could say another word, she reached down and knocked my drink over with the back of her hand. The lid popped off the Styrofoam cup, drowning my dinner in carbonated water and icy syrup. As I quickly slid over to the other end of the booth to avoid getting rained on, I noticed Amy Thompson stalking out of the restaurant without looking back once.

Well, there goes my dinner for tonight, I thought ruefully, staring down at the sopping mush on my tray. At least I had gotten the senior discount.

Therefore do not let sin reign in your mortal body, that you should obey it in its lusts. And do not present your members as instruments of unrighteousness to sin, but present yourselves to God as being alive from the dead, and your members as instruments of righteousness to God. -Romans 6:12-13

Chapter 7

The Biker

It was early morning. I had had my coffee and was busy out on my front lawn watering the flower beds. The quiet morning air was cool and peaceful. I wore my floppy gardening hat and dirt-smudged gloves, breathing in the smell of wet grass and flowers in their last bloom of the year. Even though I had gardeners who would come once a week to care for my yard, I preferred to look after the large flower bed that ran along the west side of the house myself. The evening sun would shine on the upturned faces of the flowers, and Vicki always said she could almost see them smiling in the warm sun's rays.

Vicki was the reason I wouldn't let anyone else take care of this flower bed. It was hers especially. Years ago she had planted Lantana there alongside the house, a fiery-colored native of her home state, Texas. She said being near them felt like being back home in the south. Throughout the summer they thrived in the heat, but now toward the middle of autumn the red and orange blossoms were in need of a little extra water and attention. I never failed to be out there every week to look after them. For Vicki's sake.

But with the rains we had been having lately, I had not needed to spend much time with my old friend, the garden hose, out in the yard.

This may likely be the last time I'll need to water our flowers, Vicki.

I shut off the water and stood looking at the Lantana gently waving in the breeze. The colors reminded me of a beach sunset. Their resilience in the state of Oregon, so far from home, always impressed me. I admired them a moment longer, then remembered something and checked my watch. I had an appointment I was going to be late for if I didn't get going soon. I started winding up the hose. As I was putting it away in the open garage, I heard a rumbling sound behind me. Turning around, I saw a motorcycle coming up the drive.

It was a heavy Harley Davidson bike, one of the older models that had clearly had some chopper work done on it. The bike was splattered here and there with mud, and a spidery crack divided the glass lenses of the headlight. It looked like it had seen a lot of mileage under its tires. But then I took a look at the big man riding the motorcycle, and involuntarily took a step back.

He looked pretty rough. He hadn't shaved in several days, and his hair was uncombed, or perhaps just blown around by the wind. He wore a black leather jacket, blue jeans, and heavy leather boots with silver buckles. This guy was the axiom of a stereotypical biker dude, and he could beat me to jelly easily if he wanted to.

He slowed to a stop about twenty feet away from me, balancing the bike with his feet on the driveway as he called out, "Hey, man! You Malachi Winstead?"

"That's me," I said, carefully. "Can I help you?"

"Yeah, you can!"

He kicked the bike stand into position so the old motorcycle wouldn't fall over, swung his leg over the side of it, and started to walk toward me, stumbling just a little.

He's got to be on drugs or something. How does he know my name?

The closer the man came, the less stable he appeared. I caught the strong scent of cigarette smoke rising from his clothes and skin. As he approached me, I gripped the garden hose a little bit tighter. I didn't know if I was going to need some kind of defensive weapon or not, but that hose had a metal spray head on it that would probably hurt a lot if I swung it hard enough.

He pulled out a crinkled pack of cigarettes and paused to light one before continuing his trek toward me. Not knowing what might happen, I braced myself when he stopped a few feet away. With him standing this close I could see the details of his face, the lines carved deep into the weathered brown skin, the beady brown eyes and wind-chapped lips. He looked to be in his mid-forties, maybe. He had probably spent more miles on two wheels than that old bike of his.

We eyed one another, just looking each other over for a minute. Then the biker folded his big arms across his chest. "Listen, mister," he said roughly, "you don't know me. But I know about you."

"Oh?"

He took another long drag of his cigarette before flicking it aside, grinding the ash beneath the heel of his boot. "I was told you were a decent kind of guy, a religious guy." He took one step in my direction, listing his head as he watched me. "Not only that, but you're gonna be dead soon. Is that right?"

The genuine curiosity in his cracked voice had me taken aback. How this stranger had any of this information about me at all was a mystery to me.

"I try to live my life as God expects me to," I said finally. He tapped his foot, waiting for the other answer he was after. I exhaled quietly. "And yes...it's true. I will die soon."

He had neither subtlety in his manner nor sympathy in his eyes. He just kept looking at me, almost as if my next words held a vast importance to him.

"But life won't end at death," I added, trying to gauge his thoughts. "There's–"

"That's what I'm talking about!" he blurted out, waving his arms. I stepped back again. He didn't seem to notice. "Heaven and hell," he rushed on, clearly excited. "Heaven for you...and hell is where I'm going." He turned away, hunching his shoulders.

By this time, with his slurred, strange dialogue and exaggeratedly unsteady movements, it seemed pretty obvious to me that this stranger had had one drink too many. He looked around furtively as if checking to see the coast was clear. Could I send him on his way as politely as I could or maybe call down the street to an invisible neighbor, just to turn his attention enough so I could make it inside the house?

Then he turned back to face me. "I need to talk to you," he said gruffly.

I looked around too, unsure how to respond.

What can it hurt to talk to him, Malachi?

I squared my shoulders and gave him a friendly smile. "Do you want to come in the house?"

"No!" His voice was suddenly sharp. "I'm just fine." He calmed down slightly and folded his beefy arms again. "Look, mister, no one is gonna hear this but you. Understand?"

"Sure. Let me grab a couple of chairs from the garage, ok?" I turned toward the garage, a familiar feeling growing in my mind. Why else would he be here?

I pulled out a couple of folding chairs and set them up on the front lawn. I let him sit down first. He braced both hands on the arms of his chair as if he would stand up again at any moment. He seemed less at ease and out of his element there.

"So, what is this you wanted to talk to me about?"

He rubbed his scruffy goatee and looked hard at me. "You're a good Christian man?" he blurted out.

"As I said, I do my best to be just that," I said. I vaguely wondered if he would make me swear on it, he appeared so determined to know exactly who I was.

He inched forward in his chair and bent toward me, his hands dangling over his knees. "Ok. So, about twenty years or so ago, I was a pretty rough guy, and I was part of one of the toughest gangs in the state."

I couldn't help myself. My eyebrows raised just enough for him to see, and he did.

"I'm gonna tell you what I came to say," he said abruptly. "I was part of a gang, and one night I was coming back home from a long ride. I saw a woman on the side of the road, standing next to her car. She had a flat, and the car was pulled so far off the road there was no way it could be jacked up in a ditch like that. It was pretty cold out. Getting dark, too, and started to rain a little. So I told her I'd give her a ride to the next town where she could find a tow truck."

He shifted around in his seat, not making eye contact with me, but tugging at his fingerless leather gloves.

"She agreed to come with me, but we'd only gotten a few miles down the road when the rain really started coming down hard, and I had to pull over 'cause I couldn't see the road."

He turned his head. "She sure was a pretty thing," he muttered, almost to himself.

I swallowed as an icy feeling started to snake through my stomach. This story couldn't end well, I already knew.

"I'd been drinking," he went on stoutly. "I barely felt the cold. I don't remember everything I said to her, but I do recall telling her that every girl who rode on my bike owed me something. I had a pint of whiskey with me and I offered her some. But she wouldn't take it. Well, then I got pretty mad, I guess. I just wanted to help keep her warm."

I pinched the bridge of my nose, closing my eyes as I waited for the worst.

"I lost my head," the big biker said quietly. "And...well, to make it brief I was willing but she wasn't. Afterward, she ran off into the woods and I couldn't find her. Then I figured it was better if I got on out of there. Next day there was a story in the news about a young woman being hit and killed by a truck while walking along the side of the road early in the morning not far from where I'd left her."

I leaned over my knees, squeezing my hands together and biting my lips, hard. The sick feeling in the pit of my stomach was growing.

"But you know what else the story said, mister?" he asked me. I looked up at him, and he returned my gaze. "They said she was a member of the church of Christ, and she was supposed to get married in a couple of months. They talked about having her funeral there where she went to church. And I...I was alright with that. I was alright with her being dead. Because I knew her death meant her silence, and her silence would keep me out of jail for what I did."

He did not speak as if he truly regretted what he had done, but more like he was simply stating the facts, laying the truth out bare for me to do with it what I would. As much as I was repulsed by his story, the man's raw honesty compelled me to listen to the end of it.

"The week after it happened, I joined the military," he continued. "I stayed away from there for over ten years, thinking maybe I could erase my past by running away from it. But I never stopped thinking about that girl." He folded his arms, shaking his shaggy head. "Seems like every day I remember what I did to her that caused her to lose her life. For ten years, I've tried gettin' her memory out of my head whatever way I could. But she won't let me go." He gazed off into the distance. "Just like I wouldn't let her go."

What on earth do I say to this man? My tongue was twisted in knots similar to the ones inside me.

"Look here, I hadn't never told anyone about this except you," he said, his brows furrowing fiercely. "Now I need you to do something for me."

Wondering what I could possibly do to help this wretched soul, I raised my shoulders and asked, "What is it you need?" *Besides handcuffs and a Bible?*

"I told you in the beginning I came to you 'cause you're a Christian, like that girl was. And I think it'll help my conscience if you tell her, when you take that trip upstairs," and he jabbed his finger toward the sky. "If you'll just tell that girl how sorry I am for what I'd done to her. And...and maybe if you could ask her to forgive me."

I was amazed at his temerity, but I was also aware of how this hulking, tough biker gang member was also a man desperately in need of God and forgiveness. He was just as vulnerable as every other mortal in this world. Part of me yearned to help him, but I could see he was already restless and ready to get back on his bike.

"I don't know if I will be able to do what you ask," I said. "But if I can give her your message, sir, I will."

Without a thank-you or even a nod, he stood up and walked

back toward the driveway. He had done what he came to do, and I guess he was not going to stick around another minute. I followed him back to his bike.

"You know," I said to him, raising my voice above the roar as he started up the Harley. "I'm more than willing to help you so when you die, you could maybe give that girl that message yourself."

He curled his hands around the bike handles, turning to look at me.

"No, thanks," he said. "Heaven is for people like you, not for people like me. I know where I'm headed."

With that, he revved his engine and sped down my driveway, leaving a black tire streak across the concrete.

I did my best not to break the speed limit, but I knew I was late some time before I pulled into the parking lot of the funeral home. I had always been a stickler for keeping time, and being even a few minutes late brought me more frustration than was probably rational. I stepped out of the car and walked up to the building. As I entered the funeral home, the calm atmosphere with soft lighting and low instrumental music drifting through the air soothed my agitation somewhat.

It occurred to me how very strange it was to be standing there in the foyer. After all, it isn't every day that you go pick out the coffin you are going to be buried in.

I walked up to the front desk where an elderly lady was writing something in a leather-bound appointment book. She looked up when I approached and smiled.

"Can I help you, sir?"

My gaze fell upon the image of a cross hanging on the wall behind her. "Yes. I have an appointment with Mr. Lovemore. I'm afraid I'm a bit late."

"Oh, that's quite alright, sir. Perfectly understandable. Most people who show up here are."

The black humor in her statement caused me to feel surprise, and then snicker quietly before I could stop myself,

despite the circumstances of why I was there.

"Your name, sir?"

"Malachi Winstead."

"If you'll wait just a minute, I'll let Mr. Lovemore know you're here," she promised, and picked up the phone receiver on her desk. "Mr. Lovemore," she spoke into it, "Malachi Winstead is here."

She listened for a few moments, said, "Yes sir," and hung up. She gave me a sweet smile like a mother would to her child and said in a maternal voice, "Mr. Lovemore will be right with you, Mr. Winstead."

"Thank you." I clasped my hands behind my back and looked around the room some more. There were a couple of wall tables with vases of freshly cut flowers that gave off a faint perfume, mingling with the feel of professional silence. Everything was orderly and clean. I ran my fingers along the edge of a heavy Bible with gilded pages lying open to Psalm twenty-three.

Even in the valley of the shadow of death, I will not fear, for You are with me...

"Mr. Winstead?"

A dignified, middle-aged man walked toward me, straightening his tie and the sleeves of his dark gray sports jacket. He wore a pleasant smile, and his eyes behind a black-rimmed pair of glasses were kind. I could already tell he was of a warmer personality than I had expected and felt much better about this appointment.

"Yes, I am he," I answered, stepping up to shake his hand. "I apologize for being late. I was held up, but it was for a good cause."

"No worries, Mr. Winstead." His voice was as calm and cool as the funeral home itself. "Funeral homes are usually the places we tend to show up at last-minute."

"That's what I hear." I smiled.

"So, please tell me exactly what I can do to help you today," Mr. Lovemore told me as he gestured for me to walk beside him down the hall. "I know you said you wanted to find a casket."

"Yes, that's right."

"Well, sir, if you'll just come with me I think we can find what you're looking for."

We stopped by his office where he picked up a leather folder similar to the one at the front desk, except his contained prices and order forms. Then we continued down the wide hallway, which was lighted every few feet by softly glowing lamps. The rosy carpet muffled our footsteps.

"So, Mr. Winstead," Mr. Lovemore said as he flipped through his book, "you indicated on the phone that you wanted a casket, but no funeral arrangements. That's a rather unusual request. I don't get many like that."

"Yes, Mr. Lovemore, I just want a casket."

"Of course, sir, that is up to you." He made a note with a fountain pen. "So this is for a loved one?"

I pulled up the corner of my mouth. "No. It's for me."

Mr. Lovemore tilted his head. "For you?" Then he paused and looked harder at me through his glasses. "Are you wanting something for a cremation, Mr. Winstead?" he asked quietly, his forehead wrinkling.

"No. Just a regular casket, please."

We came to the end of the hall where Mr. Lovemore opened one of the double doors. He led me into a large room with caskets arrayed along the walls and forming an aisle down the center.

"Wow," I joked as I walked around looking at the different coffins. "This is going to be a tough choice. Look at all these beautiful boxes."

I turned to see his reaction. Mr. Lovemore stood there a couple yards behind me, studying me as I walked around. I could understand if he was feeling a bit confused and decided to let him off the hook.

"I believe my son, Garrett Winstead, has an appointment to see you on Saturday to make my funeral arrangements. I just insisted on getting to pick out my own coffin," I said that last sentence with a lopsided grin.

He stared at me a moment longer, then took off his glasses,

holding the folder down by his side as he walked toward me. "Mr. Winstead, let me see if I understand. You want us to do your funeral someday, correct? You're coming in today to reserve a casket and your son is coming in this weekend to make the necessary arrangements...but you seem pretty healthy to me. I'm no doctor, but–"

"Not someday. It will be three weeks from today," I answered.

The funeral director looked even more baffled. He probably didn't get many people in his office who knew exactly when they would be back for their own funeral. Probably because most people showed up dead.

Without offering explanation, I turned and walked among the caskets, touching the silky fabrics, running my hand along the shiny, smooth handles and heavy polished wood. It was an odd sensation, standing there among all these coffins that would each eventually be the final bed of a body whose soul had taken flight into eternity. Along one wall stood a few caskets that were very small.

These little coffins caught my attention, and as I looked at them, I could hear faint, faraway cries in my ears, and images of small, still bodies lying in battle-torn fields on the other side of the world. Sights and sounds I would never be able to unsee or forget as long as I lived.

It was at least a mercy that those memories would be taken away in a short time.

Mr. Lovemore interrupted my thoughts. "Is there a price range?"

"No, just looking for the right box for my old body to fit in." I turned to face him again. "My spirit will have gone on to paradise, but I know my family and friends want to lay me to rest in a way that's comforting to them. I would have their sorrow eased however I can."

He nodded and made another note in his folder. I watched him, then said thoughtfully, "Funerals are really for the living, you know. They aren't for those of us who go on ahead."

Mr. Lovemore tucked his pen into a loop inside his folder and pursed his lips. "You're right," he remarked. "Not one of the people we put in these coffins will care what's going on around them, though people do sometimes ask us to put their cell phones in with them, or request they be buried with their favorite movie or book. I've even had somebody ask for an extra phone battery. When we're finished with them, I can guarantee they'll never use that phone they wanted in the coffin with them. But still they ask. The family makes requests like, 'My loved one wants his or her phone turned on just before you put them in the ground.' " He shrugged his shoulders. "We comply with the wishes of the family and the deceased as best we can, but there never was a truer saying than the one that goes, 'you can't take it with you.'"

I smiled at the silliness of such requests from people he had mentioned, but then sobered as I considered how naïve it really was. As I thought about it, I could feel a dull ache beginning behind my eyes. The ache started to grow, and a pounding in my head suddenly brought on a sharp wave of pain that made me lean over the coffin I stood beside, gripping the edge with whitened knuckles.

Mr. Lovemore started at my action and touched my arm. "Mr. Winstead, is something wrong? Are you alright?"

I didn't answer, just gritted my teeth and silently prayed for relief. The pain was still very sharp, and my vision was blurred by tiny white squiggly lines.

How ironic would it be if this was the coffin I chose and I just keeled over into it right now.

"Are you ok? Can I do something to help you?"

I think Mr. Lovemore was actually concerned that maybe I really would drop dead right there in front of him at his funeral parlor. I'm sure that hadn't happened to him before. I tried to pull myself together and took a deep breath, putting a hand to my eyes but keeping a grip on the coffin handle with the other.

"I'll be ok, just got a migraine. I think it's starting to ease up a little. Just give me a minute and I'll be fine." I tried to steady myself.

"Can I get you a chair or some water?"

I shook my head. "Don't trouble yourself." I inhaled deeply again, then looked up at the coffin I was holding onto. I mustered a twisted smile and patted the shiny wood. "I believe this is just the right one for me."

A few minutes later Mr. Lovemore had me sitting in a chair in his office and was offering me something to drink. "Water? Soda? Coffee?"

"If you have any coffee, I'll drink it," I said, and he left the room, soon returning with the hot drink in Styrofoam cups for both of us. He sat down behind his desk and spread out the order form, marking down the casket model I had chosen. I cupped my hands around my coffee, trying to subdue a head-splitting yawn. The fierce pounding in my head had quieted to a low throbbing, but now I was worn out.

Mr. Lovemore put down his pen and let the folder thump closed. Leaning forward, he rested his cheek on his hand. "You know, Mr. Winstead, I believe you are the first person I've ever had as a client who came in here knowing the day of their funeral."

"I guess there's a first time for everything," I said, wincing as I took a sip.

"Are you planning to commit suicide?" His voice was as calm as if he were asking the time.

"No," I said firmly. "Absolutely not. As a Christian, it would be a sin, and I would die in sin if I took my own life. No, suicide is never an option." I looked down at my feet. "No matter how bad life gets," I added in a murmur.

He folded his hands together. "Then may I ask you a question?"

"Of course."

"You seem to know what you're doing and what's going to happen to you in this life. Do you know what is going to happen to you after you die?"

"Because I am a faithful Christian, I know where I'm going, and that is to be with God," I answered peacefully. Mr. Lovemore knit his brows.

"You will have my body after I'm gone, but the Lord will have my soul. And that's all that matters."

"So you believe all people who die go on to be with God?" he asked.

"No. As sad as that is, no. God's Son, Jesus Christ, made that very clear in the Bible. Only a faithful few will go to heaven after they die. But most of the world will find themselves in hell for eternity."

He leaned back in his swivel chair, rocking it a little. "I attend many funerals in my profession. And I can tell you this, most every one of the ministers or the family members will say that they know their loved one has gone on to heaven."

I nodded. "Yes. A lot of families believe that. But Jesus said that many will one day say to Him, 'Look at all the good I have done.' And even so, the Lord said He would say to them, 'I never knew you.' "

I stood up then, wishing to be on my way. "Thank you for the coffee, Mr. Lovemore."

He stood up, too, and reached across the desk to shake my hand. "You're welcome."

A tiny smile crept over my face. "I suppose you shouldn't tell me to come back soon, eh?"

A surprised expression came over his face, then he smiled and shook his head. I turned to leave, but stopped on the threshold.

"Take good care of my body," I said softly.

"Don't worry, Mr. Winstead." His voice was strong and reassuring. "We will."

"Enter by the narrow gate; for wide is the gate and broad is the way that leads to destruction, and there are many who go in by it. Because narrow is the gate and difficult is the way which leads to life, and there are few who find it. -Matthew 7:13-14

Chapter 8

The Little Girl

Sunday morning dawned crisp and cool, another perfect autumn day. I was at the church building, sitting in my regular pew like on any other normal Sunday. The worship hour had just ended, and a number of other members stopped by or were waiting their turn to speak to me where I sat. As they shook my hand and asked me how I was doing, I noticed a sweet little girl bobbing at the end of the pew near me. She stood on one foot, then the other, evidently eager to talk to me but patiently waiting her turn. She was about six years old, with beautiful dark skin and hair tied up in pigtails with pink ribbons. After a minute, she came and sat down beside me. I knew her and gave her a smile to let her know I was aware of her presence.

When the adults had moved away from us, I turned to her and opened my arms for a hug. "Good morning, Miss Charlene. And just how are you this morning?"

She hugged me back. "Hi, Mr. Malachi!"

"I'm telling you, you sure look pretty today," I told her, and she grinned, showing her tiny pearly whites. "Thanks, Mr. Malachi! Hey, can I tell you something?"

"You know you can, sweetheart. What is it?"

"My Daddy said I should come and talk to you about it," she said seriously. I glanced up and saw her father standing a few rows over. He met my gaze and smiled, shrugging. I looked back at the little girl beside me. "Miss Charlene, why did your daddy think you needed to come talk to me?"

She tugged on one of her pigtails. "Daddy said you know

my Mama."

Ah... Now I understood.

"I did know your mother, honey. I knew her when she was just a little older than you are now. And years later I had the privilege of being there when she was baptized. And hey..." I leaned down toward her as if telling a secret. Her brown eyes were big as she listened. "I was here when your mama and daddy got married in this church building!"

"You were?" she exclaimed, looking up and all around her as if expecting to see it all happen in front of her. I smiled and nodded.

"Daddy said you'll see my Mama soon. Will you really?"

I looked at her kindly and patted her hand. "I believe that's true, sweetie."

She gasped and put both hands over her mouth. "Oh, Mr. Malachi!" She looked at me, her eyes still big as she tried to understand. I knew at her age it wasn't possible, and I was glad. Her innocence was precious.

"Mr. Malachi, will you please tell my Mama I love her?" she asked me. "Tell her I love her and miss her? I want to tell her, too, but I can't. Not til I'm really old like you, and that's too long. I don't want Mama to wait that long."

I searched for a reply, but before I could give one, Charlene hopped up, threw her arms around my neck and kissed my cheek. Then she scurried back to her father, who took her hand and gave me a grateful smile for helping his daughter.

It really is a blessing to have the ability to bring comfort to others. Not only was I hearing and reliving the sacred memories of the people who were coming to me with their messages to be carried beyond the grave, but I was discovering the lives of people who had made a significant impact on others they had known. It is true that each life affects another. Now it was for me to wonder how many more I would encounter before I left, and how many more messages I would be asked to take with me.

It was just after lunch the following Tuesday, and I was

washing up my dishes when the doorbell rang. Drying my hands on one of the towels Vicki had always made sure was hanging on the outside dishwasher handle, I went to see who was at the door.

The woman standing there when I opened it was rather heavy-set with sweatpants and a lightweight jacket of the same bright color. She wore a sweatband around the crown of her head, and her frizzy red hair was flying in every direction at once. Overall I would assume she had just been out for a jog, though judging by her new-looking sneakers she hadn't gone very far in them.

"Hey, there, are you Malachi Winstead?"

I wondered how many more times I was going to answer that question during the next couple of weeks, but she didn't let me.

"You don't know me," she rambled on, "but my name is Dorothy Higgins, and I just moved in on the next block about a week ago. It's my sister's house. She's letting me live there until I can buy a house in the area."

"Ah," I said, not sure what else to say.

She continued as if I hadn't spoken. "I've been chatting with some of your neighbors, and talking with them gave me the idea that you might be able to help me."

I thought of Dike Randal. Had he mentioned me to this woman? I couldn't imagine him recommending my help to anyone after our last conversation.

"Well, Ms. Higgins, I'm glad to meet you. I don't know if I can help you though. What is it that you need?"

"Oh, it's ok, honey," she broke in. "Your neighbor told me that you'll be gone soon, and your house may be for sale. Is that true?"

"Yes, it is true my time is short, but as for the house, you were told wrong. It isn't up for sale. In the near future, it may go on the market, but I suggest you wait for the yard sign," I added.

She answered boisterously, "Oh, well, that's alright, honey. But can I see it now?"

I wasn't sure I had heard her right. "The house? You want me to show you my house?"

She widened her eyes and nodded as if it was the easiest thing in the world to comprehend.

Is she for real?

I shook my head. "Ms. Higgins, I don't think now is a good time for that. Again, I think you need to wait until you see the sign out front."

My last few words were clipped, and I could feel another headache coming on.

"Are you feeling ok, Malachi?" Irritation flared up inside me at her casual use of my first name, coupled with her sudden concern that seemed mainly curiosity because my issues were standing in the way of what she wanted.

"I just have a headache." I leaned against the doorjamb, hoping maybe the hint would drive her away. "I think it's getting worse."

"Oh, my Chuck had horrible headaches," she said quickly. "It was the brain tumor that caused them before he died."

"It's not a tumor. I'm really allergic to ragweed this time of year." I massaged my forehead.

"Well then, honey, can I ask you another question?"

My patience was running thin and my reluctance high. My headache wasn't letting up, and I was wishing she would go away of her own accord. However, I didn't want to be rude, and maybe there was some way I could be of help to her.

"Sure, go ahead," I said, shutting my eyes.

"Ok, honey. Your neighbor said you were a Christian. Is that right?"

"I do my best to honor Christ by wearing His name–"

"Good, good," she interrupted again. "Then you'll be seeing my Chuck in heaven."

"Oh, I will?" I opened my eyes. "I hope I do. Was he a Christian?"

"Oh, yes. Both of us," she said proudly.

"That's good. What church congregation do you attend?"

"Well, you see, Malachi, our lives have always been very busy. We didn't have enough time for regular church, but we did go every Christmas and Easter." She beamed like she had won an Academy Award.

"I see. Well can I ask you a question?"

"Surely, surely!" she said, still smiling.

"Can you tell me how you know that your husband is in paradise?"

She looked at me like I couldn't understand something extremely obvious. "We were both saved when we were young and first married."

"Is that so," I muttered, feeling my temples throbbing.

"Yes, we both took Jesus into our hearts and then we knew that we were saved," she said emphatically.

"But how do you know your husband was saved when he died?" I persisted.

She leaned toward me, her voice dropping almost to a whisper, though there was nobody else around to hear. "Malachi, hon, we always knew. Everyone knows that once you're saved, you're always saved!" She pulled back and stuffed some of her flyaway hair back under her sweatband. "So that's how I know that my Chuck and I will be together in heaven forever, no matter what happens."

I took off my glasses and rubbed my forehead again.

"Ms., uh, Ms..."

"Higgins."

"Yes, Ms. Higgins, excuse me. Nowhere in the Word of God has He ever said that once a person is saved they are saved forever. If you look in the Bible, it teaches over and over that not all who become Christians will remain so. There is a stipulation that those of us who are children of God must remain faithful followers of Him to the end of our lives if we expect to go to heaven. And most people won't. Most will be lost. It is God alone Who decides those of us who are saved and those who aren't. And those people who belong to Him believe in Him and His Son Jesus. They repent of their sins, confess Jesus is Lord, are baptized for the remission of their sins, and then faithfully serve and worship God as He commands us."

I took out my wallet and handed her a card from it. "On this card is the name of a church and the preacher there who can help you. I know him personally. Please go see him. He will be more than glad to help you know what you need to do to be right with God."

She stared down at the card in her hand, then at me.

"You're kidding, right?" she said.

"I'm very serious."

She pulled her sunglasses down over her eyes. "You know what I think? I think you're just a stupid old man who doesn't have the love of Jesus in his heart. You're a hypocrite and a liar. God wants everyone to be saved."

With that, she tossed the card away and walked off. I let the screen door fall to and went back into the kitchen, thinking back over the conversation.

"God wants everyone to be saved." *How true what she said. Yet how sad that she doesn't understand what God wants her to know so she can be.*

He who finds a wife finds a good thing,
And obtains favor from the Lord. -Proverbs 18:22

Chapter 9

Vicki

I checked my emails and phone messages every morning, and there were more than ever now as my time grew short. I was in the midst of reading a long email a couple of mornings after my last strange encounter, when my doorbell rang. Surely it couldn't be Ms. Higgins again, come back to try to get a tour of the house. I got up and answered the door.

I was surprised to see a beautiful young woman standing there who looked to be in her early twenties. She wore her long golden-brown hair in curly ringlets, tied back in a bow, and the angles of her heart-shaped face were soft, like her brown eyes. She wore bright red lipstick and was dressed in heels, a black skirt, and a red blouse with a black jacket. She held a laptop case in one hand.

"Hello," she said brightly when I opened the door. She pulled back a loose strand of hair the wind blew into her eyes. "You're Malachi Winstead."

She didn't pose it like a question but seemed to know with confidence that I was the person she was looking for.

"You've found me," I said, and she quickly held out her hand.

"I'm Sandy Reynolds," she introduced herself as we shook hands. Her grip was firm. "Now, I know you have no idea who I am, but I know that you did know my aunt, Maggie Reynolds."

Her self-assurance was impressive. I thought for a second, then smiled. "Oh, yes, I remember sister Maggie very well. She's a very sweet, very special lady. Known her many, many years."

Sandy cocked her head. "May I come in?"

"Well, I–"

She smiled and marched straight past me into the entryway of my house. I turned to comprehend what had just happened and saw her looking all around with interest.

"You have a beautiful home," she commented gaily. "My aunt said you were a widower. You must have a housekeeper if your home is this well-kept."

She walked into the adjoining dining room and set her case down on the table, comfortable as if she lived here. I followed her and found her pulling out some papers and arranging them carefully on the table.

"You do remember my aunt telling you about the book I'm writing, don't you?" she said without looking up. I stood by my chair at the head of the table, watching her and wondering why she was here. In my house. Turning my dinner table into a work desk.

"Um, I guess I do remember your aunt telling me something about her niece writing something," I hedged, trying to remember exactly what Maggie Reynolds had told me the last time I had seen her. I thought I recalled her saying something about somebody in her family writing a book...

"It's not just an ordinary book about anything," Sandy said quickly. "It's a book about marriage."

She stepped back for a moment to study her arrangements. "Hmm."

"But your aunt never said anything about you coming here," I said in the kind of tone that usually nudges the question that needs answering. Sandy, however, was unperturbed.

"Well, she called me and said I should probably come over here and see you now because I may not get the chance to later." She picked up a pen and clicked it a couple of times. "Is that alright? Do you have time for an interview this morning, Mr. Winstead? It would mean an awful lot to me if you do, an awful lot!"

I couldn't help but smile at her earnestness. "Certainly, I have the time, but just what kind of interview are you talking about?"

She held up a paper with bold black lettering in huge font that read, "Great and Godly Marriages for the Christian Couple to Aspire To" and underneath in smaller letters, "By Sandy Reynolds".

"Kind of a long-winded title, isn't it?" I commented, teasing her just a little. She lowered the paper and sighed.

"I know it is. This is my motivation page. You see, whenever I start a new writing project, I type out the title and my name under it, kind of like it would look if it were a real book cover, you know? Then I hang it on the wall wherever my writing space is, so I can look up and see it, and it inspires me to keep on going." She laid the paper carefully back in the briefcase. "I've been meaning to tweak this title a little when I get more of the book written. I'm hoping maybe interviewing you will give me some more ideas!" she finished with an eager smile.

"Well now, that's a pretty good idea." I folded my arms. "But what makes you think I had a great marriage that would be suitable for your book?"

Sandy straightened up. "My aunt said all the ladies in the church who knew you and your wife believe that you had one of the best relationships and marriages ever. I couldn't pass up an opportunity to talk to you about that!"

I hadn't talked about Vicki and myself in detail to anyone in a long time. But the idea of opening up about my marriage to this young stranger, so eager to write her book, gave me a sudden sense of excitement myself. After all, I had had the best marriage of anybody alive. To have it written about, possibly for the world to one day know, pleased me greatly. Besides, everyone should know about Vicki.

"Ok," I said to Sandy. "What is it that you would like to know?"

She beamed from ear to ear. I was reminded of the look on my granddaughter's face when I gave her my red sports car for her graduation. That same joy and excitement was there.

"Just let me finish getting set up here...it won't take a minute!" She raced back to the table and pulled out her laptop,

opened it, and plugged the charger into the wall outlet.

"Would you like some tea this morning?" I offered. "I can make some for us if you like."

"I like tea!" she declared, typing a password into the laptop. "But I'll only drink it hot. I've never liked cold tea, from the time I was little. My family thinks I'm weird for that, but they love me anyway," she laughed. I liked her carefree, easy-going attitude. I went into the kitchen and started making the tea. I heard Sandy starting to hum to herself in the next room. It brought another smile to my face. I missed having the grandkids over, with their singing all over the house.

You'll soon be hearing even better singing than that, old boy.

I set the kettle on to boil and walked back into the dining room, where she was sitting behind her laptop, fingers poised to start typing. "So, tell me again just what do you want to know about my marriage?"

She scanned the page of questions she had on the table, then looked up at me, her large eyes dreamy. "Was it love at first sight?"

I chuckled and pulled out the chair across from her. "No, it wasn't. But it all started when I was beginning a new life. Vicki, before she was my wife, worked as a part-time secretary for the church congregation where I was visiting and learning all I could about becoming a Christian. I would go visit with the preacher in his study at the church building every day at the start, and he gave me plenty of Bible material to study and read along with the Bible to help grow my faith."

Sandy's fingers flew over the laptop keys. Keeping an ear out for the tea kettle whistle, I went on.

"The first couple of days, I had to wait in the church office until the preacher was done meeting with somebody else. Vicki was sitting across the room behind the desk, and I tell you..." My gaze drifted away into another time. "The more I looked at this beautiful woman with her fiery red hair and big green eyes, the more interested I became in her."

Sandy looked up intently. "Was she the most beautiful woman you ever saw?"

"Indescribably so. But not only was she beautiful, she seemed very secure and confident in herself. I learned she had been a widow for a few years, and there was an age gap of almost ten years between us with me being the older one, but that didn't bother me."

I heard the kettle whistle, and went to pour us each a mug of hot tea. When I was settled back in my chair again and Sandy alert and waiting, I went on.

"Vicki would always offer me coffee when I came in, and I made small talk with her while waiting for the preacher. The first day, I asked him about her, and he told me she was a widow. When I learned that it had been a long, long time since her husband's death, I asked her the next day if I could take her out to lunch, or dinner."

"And did she say yes?" Sandy demanded.

I smiled in remembrance. "She looked at me with those lovely green eyes of hers and said in the sweetest voice you can imagine, 'No, I don't think so.'"

Sandy made a sputtering noise into her tea. "What! She said no?"

"Yes, she sure did. So I asked the preacher if there was someone she was seeing, and he said not that he knew of, so I couldn't figure out why she would say no. Being the naïve man that I was, I assumed she had no reason in the world for turning me down." I smiled at the memory. "But for the next week, every time I came in, Vicki would offer me coffee, and I always asked, 'Lunch or dinner today?' And she always smiled sweetly and said, 'No, I don't think so.' Well, after a couple weeks or so of Bible study, I had my mind made up that my life would forever be different from what it had been before, and that I wanted to repent and God would forgive me for all I had done. I wanted Jesus to be my Lord and Savior, so I determined to become a new person in Him. I told the preacher I couldn't wait, so on that very day he baptized me for the remission of my sins. I became a Christian with my heart

set on doing what was right from then on."

I saw Sandy smiling to herself as she typed away. "So what happened with you and Vicki then?" she asked.

"The evening of the day I became a Christian, the preacher invited me over to his home for dinner. As we sat around the table with his family, the conversation turned to Vicki. 'I haven't been able to get her off my mind since I first saw her. I just can't stop thinking about her,' I told the preacher and his wife. 'And I can't understand how, while she's always kind and considerate toward me, she won't give me the time of day. Just a cup of coffee.' I remember the preacher and his wife looked at each other and smiled. I wanted to know what they meant by that smile, and that's when the preacher told me, 'Well you see, Malachi, Vicki sat across from us in that same place, where you are now, just last night, and told Becky and I nearly the exact same thing.'"

"I was shocked. 'What do you mean? She likes me?'"

"The preacher's wife said, 'All the time we've known her after the death of her husband, Vicki has never shown interest in anyone like she shows interest in you.'"

"Well, you can imagine how that lit up my world. But at the same time, I was so confused, because of how Vicki had been treating me. Why would she refuse to go on a date with me if she liked me the way I liked her? It didn't make sense. I told the preacher and his wife this, and they smiled at each other again, in that little way they had, and then he told me, 'Malachi, Vicki would never go out with, or date any man who wasn't a Christian.'"

"Well, I had never thought about it like that. I didn't know what to think. As much as I loved the Lord, Christianity was still very fresh and new to me. But then I remembered, hey, now I am a Christian. So I asked the preacher if he would be willing to call Vicki for me and ask if it would be alright if I came to see her. He said he would, though he warned me he couldn't promise anything for certain. Then he walked into the other room to make the call on his phone."

"Were you very nervous?" Sandy asked with a grin. I could tell she was eating up every word of this modern day romance.

"I was sweating and panicking and shaking, if that's what you mean by 'nervous'," I said with a chuckle. "It felt like that preacher would never come back, but he did. I was helping his wife clear the table. I remember I was holding a china gravy boat when he came over to me and held up a piece of paper with Vicki's address and phone number on it. He was smiling, and all he said was, 'I think it'll take you about ten minutes to get there.'" I smiled now at the memory. "I'll be forever grateful to that preacher and his wife. Not only for bringing Vicki and me together, but for being so gracious about the mess I made when I dropped their gravy boat on the floor and nearly broke it."

Sandy giggled softly. "What happened then? Did you go straight to Vicki's house?"

"Straight to Vicki's house. She was sitting on the front porch waiting for me, like in a movie. I asked if she wanted to go get some coffee with me."

"Like she had offered you coffee so many times!"

"Exactly. So the two of us went to a Denny's down the road, and sat across from each other in a small booth. We had coffee and stayed there talking long after midnight. Two months later we were married."

"Only two months!" Sandy exclaimed, wrinkling her forehead. "Such a short time."

"It was all the time Vicki and I needed to realize that we wanted to spend the rest of our lives together," I said quietly, draining the last of my tea.

Sandy typed a few more words, then flexed her fingers. She folded her arms and looked at me, pursing her lips in thought. "So, just what was it that made your marriage so great?"

I set my cup on the table and turned it slowly round and round. "I didn't say my marriage was always great and that everything that happened was always good, but God did say that if a man finds a good wife, then she would be a gift from God. I truly believe Vicki was my godsend. I was blessed to have the best wife there ever was. We were one, but she was the better half. I couldn't have done it without her. She was the love of my life every single

day, and I only fell more in love with her every single day."

"What made your time together the best there ever was?"

I stopped turning the cup and looked over at the picture on the wall of a much younger man than I was now standing beside a lovely woman with fiery red hair, both smiling and waving for the camera.

"Vicki was...my best friend. She cared for me more than anything else, and more importantly, she was determined to take me to heaven with her. When you find a person like that, you can't ask for anyone better. We were a team. She helped me grow beyond the sins that had been in my life to become the Christian man the Lord wanted me to be." I stopped, feeling the emotions come. "She was just a good, good woman. The Lord always came first in her life. Then it was me, then our children. But I was never jealous, because I knew that it was our love for God that kept us strong and kept us holding onto each other during the toughest of times."

"A team," Sandy repeated thoughtfully. "I like that."

"She let me be the man I needed to be, and the husband God expected me to be. She was beautiful inside and out." I was almost stumbling over my words trying to express myself. "God blessed us to be able to work together from the beginning in the church and in the building of our own business. Vicki managed a great home for us and our children. Later, we would be blessed financially to travel the world on mission trips. The Lord took care of us, and everything worked out according to His will for our life together."

I slowed down and sat in silence while the sound of Sandy's rapid typing click-clacked throughout the room. She took a long gulp of tea and set the empty mug on the table with a contented sigh.

"Can I get you some more tea? I think I also have some cake in the kitchen if you would like some."

"More tea would be great. It's a little too early for cake, though."

I refilled our tea cups and we resumed our interview.

"What were the little things that made your marriage special?" Sandy asked, drawing her pen through another question on her list.

"What made it special?" I smiled. "Everything about Vicki was special. We were both morning people, but I was always up first, so I put the coffee on. Then after a little while I would say to her, 'Are you ready to get up?' And she would say, 'No, I can't get out of bed without my cup of coffee first.' I loved to spoil her. She knew I would always bring her coffee in bed."

"That's sweet," Sandy said gently.

My smile faded as I looked over to the fireplace in the corner of the dining room. My eyes traveled up to the mantle where, propped up against the silver-framed picture of Vicki, stood a perfect, round sand dollar. My vision started to grow a little blurry and my eyes grew hot.

"I believe with all my heart that Vicki was the best the Lord had," I said with a catch in my voice. "But she would only be mine for twenty-four years before He decided to take her home to Him."

Sandy's typing faltered, then stopped. I could feel her watching me uncomfortably, perhaps wondering if my emotions would become too much for me. I sighed and gave her a slight smile.

"It's alright. Vicki and I will be together again soon. It's one of the things I look forward to the most."

Sandy folded her hands and rested her chin on them. "That was a very good story," she said slowly. "And I think that's a perfect place to end it." She closed her laptop, stood up, and began putting her things back into the case. I picked up our mugs and took them into the kitchen. When Sandy had everything packed up, I walked to the front door with her.

"Thank you so much for the story," she told me sincerely as she shook my hand in farewell. "It will make a wonderful chapter in my book. I appreciate you opening up about your marriage. You really did have a lovely one."

I nodded and opened the door for her, watching to see that

she made it back to her car. She made her way across the front porch and onto the first step, then turned around as if remembering something she had forgotten to say.

"Your wife..." she began, but stopped. I knew what was on her mind.

"It was a brain tumor," I answered.

Sandy stood still for several seconds. Then she gave one very slow nod and headed back down the porch steps.

Just after seven o'clock, I had finished my sandwich and sat down to enjoy a bowl of ice cream along with the evening news. I had barely taken my first bite of cold, creamy goodness when my phone rang. I had to swallow so fast that I got a mini-brain freeze as I picked up.

"Hello?"

"Malachi, this is Carrie Stevenson," said a gentle, caring voice that only took me a second to recognize as one of the sisters in the congregation with which I worshiped.

"Hello there, sister! How are you?" I said kindly, shifting my ice cream bowl onto the coffee table.

"I'm doing alright, thank you. But Malachi, I was wondering if maybe I could drop by and talk with you tonight. It'll only take a few minutes, if that's ok. I'm already out and about running errands or I wouldn't intrude on you–"

"You come right over," I told her. "How soon do you think you'll be here?"

"Ten minutes, maybe?"

"Perfect. I have a little time to dust the chandelier," I joked.

A short while later, I heard a quick knock at the door, and hurried to open it. Carrie Stevenson stood there and immediately said, "I'm so sorry for any inconvenience from this unplanned meeting." I waved it all away, happy to see her. She was not only a busy wife and mother of three children, but helped coordinate the youth activities at church, as well as being one of the Bible class teachers. Carrie was just the sort of person who everyone admired, with her sweet temper and kind spirit.

"So what are you doing here, Carrie?" I asked as I offered her a seat in the living room. "Can I get you anything to drink, by the way?"

"You're very kind, but no." She tugged off the scarf from around her neck and wadded it up in her hands, then stretched it back out again. "Malachi, I just had to talk to you, and tonight was the only chance I could get. Are you certain you can spare a few minutes?"

"Sure, Carrie. I'm glad you came. Is everything ok at home? Is that husband of yours treating you alright?" I could still sense nervousness in her.

"Tim treats me wonderfully, Malachi. He has to leave town very early in the morning so he went to bed early tonight."

"And the boys, how are they doing?"

"I left them at home studying for their finals tomorrow." She gave a lopsided smile. "I just hope when I come back that they'll still be where I left them. I told them I was going to the store, which is where I'll be going after I leave here, but I didn't tell them I was stopping by to see you." She buried her hands into the plum-colored fabric of the heavy scarf in her lap. "I need to tell you something, Malachi. Something I've never told anyone, not my family, my husband, or my children. But now I know that I must tell you."

"Are you sure you want to tell me?" I asked her. "If this is something that you haven't even told Tim, then I might think about the wisdom–"

"Oh, please, Malachi," she begged in agitation. "When I tell you, you'll understand the reasons why I've kept it a secret from everyone for so long. Please."

I looked into her troubled face and decided I would do my best to help a sister in Christ. "Alright, Carrie. If you really think you need to tell me something, you go ahead."

She looked down at her lap and took a deep breath, gathering her thoughts. "You know I was raised in the church. I was baptized at an earlier age, and throughout my teen years did my best to stay faithful in everything I did. In college I worked very hard, and was at the top of my class. I never attended any of the parties the dorms were having all the time because I was so focused on my studies."

"Which is what college is about, but many don't see it that way," I remarked.

"Yes. Well, something happened over the summer before my senior year. My roommate talked me into going to a smaller get-together with some of the other students. I usually said no, but I just felt so tired of studying and thought a break would be refreshing. My roommate told me it would be just fine and that I would meet some really nice people whom she thought highly of. I didn't think it would be like one of the huge, crazy parties, and that we would only stay a little while anyway, so I caved and said yes. Besides, my roommate knew I didn't drink or do any of the other immoral things that went on around us on the campus. So I went out with her. But at that party...somebody put something in my coke."

Carrie put her head in her hands. "I had no idea. I didn't think it would be that kind of party. Or maybe I just wanted to believe that. The next thing I remember was that I woke up in the back of a car in the parking lot the next morning. It was then I knew that something horrible had happened, but not knowing exactly what was absolutely terrifying."

"Carrie, you don't have to tell me this," I broke in, but she talked over me.

"Yes I do, Malachi. Please let me finish." She closed her eyes tightly for a second. "Two months later, I knew I was pregnant. What could I do? What would my parents think? I didn't want to imagine their disappointment, not to mention what everyone else back home would think of me. I knew I couldn't have a baby and finish school too. My senior year was coming up, and if I quit now there would be no graduation and I would be without a job. Worst of all, I couldn't even explain what had happened, or who the father was. And somehow I knew that nobody would believe that. I felt so stupid, ashamed, and afraid."

I folded my hands and asked quietly, "What did you do

with the baby, Carrie?"

She didn't answer me for what seemed like a long time. I could see her mouth working as she fought back tears. "I found an ad for a place, not far from the school campus. I read that they could make all my problems go away. So I went there and took the free test just to make certain. I tested positive for pregnancy. And the people there knew how to talk to me. They told me it was simply a mass of lifeless tissue that in a few minutes could be easily taken care of without anyone ever even knowing it had been there." She wiped her eyes, her voice starting to shake. "They told me that what had happened to me wasn't my fault, so why let this ruin my life? So, in a moment of weakness and fear, I decided that in an hour or two it could all be over and I would get my life back."

Carrie looked at me with her eyes full of tears. I knew her tender heart was breaking.

"Malachi," she sobbed, "I did get my life back, but for the past twenty years I have carried the knowledge that I helped murder an innocent human being. I destroyed the life inside me because of my own selfishness and fear. Oh, my poor baby!"

She covered her face again and cried. I moved over to where I was sitting next to her and rubbed her shoulder. "Carrie," I said gently, "if you repented of this, you know God has forgiven you."

"I know," she whispered, trying to quiet her sobs. Her shoulders heaved a couple more times, as her breathing quieted. "I just can't forgive myself, Malachi. And I knew that you were the one I had to tell about this because I know you will be in paradise soon, and I wanted to ask if you would give my sweet unborn baby a message from his or her mother. Tell my baby..." she inhaled deeply and covered her mouth for a moment. "Ask my baby to please forgive me. And...and that I love him…."

"If I am able to give such a message, Carrie, you know I will do that for you," I told her. She looked up at me gratefully, then reached over and gave me a hug.

"Thank you," she whispered in my ear. "Lord willing, I

will see my baby someday."

"You will," I said.

Now the works of the flesh are evident, which are: adultery, fornication, uncleanness, lewdness, idolatry, sorcery, hatred, contentions, jealousies, outbursts of wrath, selfish ambitions, dissensions, heresies, envy, murders, drunkenness, revelries, and the like; of which I tell you beforehand, just as I also told you in time past, that those who practice such things will not inherit the kingdom of God. -Galatians 5:19-21

Chapter 10

The Preacher

As the days grew colder and shorter, I began walking through the neighborhood every day to a little park about a mile and a half beyond my house. Sometimes I would sit there on a bench and listen to the wind rustling through the tops of the fir trees, with the sounds of the city in the distance, and watch the squirrels hide their acorns away.

With only a few pleasant outings left to me, I decided about the middle of October to go on one of my walks before lunch. I put on my heavy jacket and wrapped a scarf around my throat before venturing out into the brisk autumn air. Though the wind nipped my nose and cheeks, I smiled. This was my kind of weather.

I saw my neighbor across the street working in his yard. He saw me, too, and after exchanging waves, he set down his rake and walked over to me. I met him on the sidewalk.

"Mr. O'Connell, how are you this fine morning?" I asked as I stuck out a gloved hand. He shook it with a smile.

"Oh, I'm doing as well as I can, Mr. Winstead," he replied. We knew each other well enough to be on first name basis, but we sometimes greeted each other formally out of fun. "Just raking up all these leaves that had the audacity to flood my lawn. But the real question is, how are you doing?"

"Doing ok, sir. Doing ok. I love this kind of weather. Fall has always been my favorite time of year," I said.

He nodded. "Sure is a pretty time of year, all the leaves changing color..." We stood looking up at the trees around us for a minute, breathing in the cold air. Then he cleared his throat.

"Ah, Malachi, do you have a minute? I'd like to talk to you."

"Sure, Rob, ok." I tucked my hands up beneath my arms.

"Well, a number of us in the neighborhood know about your situation, and that you won't be with us much longer."

I saw he felt uncomfortable talking on the subject and tried to ease it for him. "Well, nobody lives forever, Rob. But how can I help you?"

He scratched his ear. "Do you know my wife, Helen? She died about a year and a half ago of a stroke?"

"Of course I remember her, Rob. She was a sweet lady."

"Thank you. Well, she and I weren't very religious people, but I asked the preacher from the Christian Fellowship Church to do her funeral. I think he visited her a few times in the hospital for surgery just before the stroke. Anyway, I asked him to officiate, so he did. And during the funeral, he said how Helen's family had told him how good a woman she was, how wonderful a wife and mother she was, how she worked to help others who were in need, and so much more."

"I'm sure all of it was true," I said.

"It was, it was. But see, the preacher also talked a lot about heaven and how wonderful it is, and that for sure my Helen is now resting in the arms of the angels. I've been thinking a lot about what that preacher said ever since the funeral and thought if there is a God, Helen must be there with him. I've been wanting to speak with you and ask you to give Helen a message for me."

"Rob, I don't know–"

"I need you to tell her I love her." His voice trembled. "And I think about her every single day. Life is just… just so hard without her, Malachi. You know. You know."

I bowed my head. "Yes, I do know, Rob. It is hard. And it hurts. I couldn't be more sorry for your loss. I knew when I lost my wife a few years ago that the pain would never completely heal. I knew I would just have to learn how to live differently than I did before and thank the Lord for those memories left behind. The loss will always be there, Rob, but you do have to eventually move forward."

"Yes, yes, you're right. But will you give Helen my

message, Malachi? I would be so grateful."

"Rob," I said slowly, "I'm very sorry, but the preacher who did your wife's funeral was not truthful in what he said."

Rob stared at me, and I could tell he did not understand. "What do you mean?"

"From what you said, and from the little time I knew her, I'm sure Helen was a very good woman. But just being a good person will not get you into heaven. God said that heaven is only for those who have obeyed the commandments He has given us. And those things required of us to reach heaven are found in the words God has given us through His son."

"But the preacher said God loves everyone!" Rob interrupted angrily. "He said everyone would go to heaven."

"It is true that God loves everyone, but He also gives every person the right to choose to follow Jesus or follow the devil. God made heaven for those who do His will through His son, Christ."

Rob held up a hand for me to stop. "Are you some kind of preacher or priest?" he demanded.

"I'm just a Christian man trying to follow God," I said.

"Well, I'd rather believe the preacher," he said sternly. "He knows what he's talking about. He said my Helen is in heaven, and that's good enough for me. I don't need your help."

He turned and walked back to his yard where he began raking leaves anew with a ferocity that made me fear for the grass on his lawn. Sorrowful over his bitterness and the hurt that I knew he was feeling, I left him alone with his grieving thoughts.

The following afternoon, I took a frontage road off the highway that soon split off onto older road leading me to a small country church building. The parking lot was little more than packed earth from which most of the grass had been cleared or tramped down.

I parked near the door, got out and stood simply looking at the humble building. This would be the last time I would see it. This tiny church building had played a part in some of the most historical, key events in my life. I looked at the curved, wooden front doors and saw myself and Vicki exiting through them, laughing and holding hands while friends and family tossed rice at us. I walked inside. The church had one narrow center aisle with a strip of carpet, and maybe thirty pews total. I walked down the aisle, recalling the baptisms, weddings and funerals of loved ones held there over the years. The faces of those who had gone on before me especially stole my thoughts. Gazing out the window, I could see my children, running and playing outside with the other kids after worship. I remembered Vicki and me standing together, sharing a songbook as we lifted our voices in praise to God with the rest of the congregation.

Approaching the small platform and pulpit at the front, I remembered my beloved Vicki's coffin as it lay in front of the congregation before being taken out through the side door and placed in a long, black hearse.

Just a few more days now, and it'll be me they carry out of those same doors.

I ran my hand along the edge of the podium and patted it. A broad smile appeared as I thought about the countless times I had been given the honor and privilege of coming to this place to worship the true and living God.

I opened one of the other side doors and walked down a short, tiny hall to the preacher's study on the end with a nameplate reading Glenn Hoffman. The door was ajar, and I knocked twice.

"Come on in!" a man said, and as I did so he added, "I thought I heard somebody come in and since it's almost time... How are you, Malachi?"

Glenn Hoffman got up from his desk and made his way over to shake my hand and give me a hug. He was shorter than I and had to reach up to embrace me and give me a pat on the back.

"It's really good to see you, brother," he said with genuine joy in his face. "I'm so glad you could come by."

"It's good to see you too, Glenn. And it's not a problem. We have some business to go over," I said as I took a seat near his desk. He placed his fingertips together and studied me.

"Malachi, I would have been more than happy to come to

your home for this."

"I know, Glenn, but I needed to be out and taking care of business today. I still have some last things I need to do."

With concern in his eyes beneath bushy gray eyebrows, he leaned on the edge of his desk and folded his arms. "How are you doing?"

"I'm ok," I said steadily. "Just dealing with life one day at a time."

He nodded. "Well, can I get you anything to drink before we get started?"

"No thanks. It's past ten o'clock, so no more coffee for me today," I said, and he smiled.

"Now, Malachi," he began, "you asked me to do your funeral, and I want you to know I consider it an honor, but there are a few things I need to talk to you about."

"Of course."

"I have talked with Garrett and Dave about how the funeral will be conducted, but I need to know if there are any special things you would like me to do or say?"

I reached into my coat pocket and drew out a folded sheet of paper. "I've written down a few things," I said. He took it from me and unfolded it.

"Closed casket, ok. Oh, I like your list of songs, very good. I always like Our God He Is Alive for funerals, though I guess most people don't consider it to really be a funeral song."

"I think there's nothing more appropriate at the funeral of a Christian than to remind people that our Creator is still in control and alive, and that He's the One we'll be spending eternity with," I said.

"Very true, very true." His eyes scanned down over the rest of my notes. "Well, that seems to be all the information I need. But Malachi," and a little smile came over his face. "You know that not only have you been a faithful Christian, but an Elder, too. You've gone on mission trips for the church all over the globe, you've taught the gospel to hundreds of people throughout the years. You've helped to support countless good works around the world, and yet..." He tapped the paper. "You didn't mention any of those things."

I looked away, embarrassed.

"All I know is that the Lord has blessed me more than most men. To whom He has given much, He will require much. We can't do everything, but we can do the best we can with what we have."

Glenn folded up my list again and put it in his pocket. "Well on another note, you do know there is a growing list of people who want to speak at your funeral."

I smiled fondly. "Well, I can't keep them out. I won't be here, so they can say whatever they want. I just hope it's for their own and my family's benefit."

"Many people think very highly of you, Malachi," said Glenn seriously. "Myself included."

"I understand, and I'm flattered, but what is most important is what God will say about me in a few days."

"Amen, brother. But listen, you have lived nearly eighty-two years. What would you say was the most important or greatest thing in your life?" he asked.

I thought about that for a few seconds, turning over in my mind all the events I had relived over the past few weeks.

"It's true God has blessed me greatly," I said. "But I would say that the most important thing, not only in my life but in every life, is the fact that Jesus gave His life for all of us. And to learn that truth and live my life as He would have me to is the most important thing I could ever do because in a few days I will begin a new life in a new place where I will be forever with the one Who died for me."

"You're right," Glenn said. "There is no better gift than the one the Lord gave us." He stood up and patted his pocket where my notes were. "Well Malachi, I think that covers everything I need to know. Is there anything else you can think of?"

I shook my head. "No, but thank you, Glenn. For doing this for me and my family. You've been a good friend to me. I couldn't ask for better."

He gave me a sad smile that said more than words ever could. We shook hands and embraced once more. I started for the door, but had a second thought.

"Oh, Glenn, there is one more thing. I ordered five hundred copies of the DVD, *Where Do We Go When We Die*. I'd like one to be given to each person who comes to my funeral. Can you see to that?"

"Yes. Absolutely. I will make sure that happens," he promised. I thanked him again and said I better let him get back to the sermon he was writing, but suddenly he rose from his chair again and asked me to wait.

"Now, you're sure you're ok, Malachi?"

"Yes, I'm fine."

"Then could I ask you one more thing before you go?"

"You know you can, brother."

"You remember Brenda and me having a second son who was killed many years ago. He was only six years old, but that car accident took his life." Glenn had difficulty speaking calmly, and I nodded sympathetically.

"Yes, I remember that."

"I would ask you, for Brenda and myself, that when you get to paradise, you would give our son, Travis, a message for us."

I looked at Glenn and knew that his little boy would be where I was going, and put my hand on his arm.

"I will tell him whatever you need me to say, Glenn, if I am indeed allowed to."

"Thank you, Malachi," he said fervently. "If you could tell him that his mother and I both love him very much, and we can't wait to, to see him again and be with him..." He trailed off, swallowing hard. I squeezed his arm and then patted it.

"I know your request comes from your heart," I said. "I hope I can give Travis the message you want him to hear."

"I'll walk you out," he told me. Without another word, the two of us made our way back through the quiet church building as the ghosts of memories past watched us silently from the faded pews.

This is a faithful saying: For if we died with Him, We shall also live with Him. If we endure, We shall also reign with Him. If we deny Him, He also will deny us. -II Timothy 2:11-12

Chapter 11

The Birthday Party

My alarm clock woke me up at six o'clock on the hour. I reached out for the snooze button and rolled over to see the dim outline of morning light trying to get around the heavy curtains at my window. I slid out from beneath the warm covers and stretched. Then I remembered what day it was.

Today was October fifteenth. My birthday. *I am eighty-two years old today.*

I went downstairs and started my morning coffee. I turned on the news to see the events of the day. I showered, shaved, and got dressed, just following my normal morning routine. After my first cup of coffee I went outside to check on the Lantana, and even though I had just watered them I turned on the hose for one more sprinkling.

A neighbor driving to work rolled down his window and called out happy birthday to me as he went by. A few minutes later, a woman from down the street with her two children walking past stopped by my fence to wish me a happy birthday, and her children did the same, waving at me. I smiled and waved in response to all of them.

Shortly afterward I got a phone call from my sweet granddaughter who was away at college. "Hey, Grandpa! I knew you would be up and around long before my classes started, so I just wanted to call and wish you a happy birthday, and tell you I love you!"

"Thanks, sweetheart. I love you too. How's that car running for you?"

At that moment, a pickup pulled into the driveway, and I realized I would have to cut the call short. I hated to since this was the last time I would talk to my granddaughter on the phone. A lump rose in my throat as I told her I would have to go. I knew she was starting to cry too, so we made our farewell short and sweet. The last thing I heard her say was, "I'll see you soon, just like we promised."

A couple of young men from church were in the truck, which was loaded with folding tables and chairs. They jumped out and greeted me with enthusiasm. I envied them their energy.

"Brother Glenn asked us to bring these by and get them set up in your backyard for the party this afternoon," they told me. "He said you'd be up early."

"Early to bed, early to rise," I quipped, and after thanking them for bringing over the furniture, I directed them to the backyard gate.

When the boys had finished their task and gone, I went back inside and picked up my car keys. Then my phone rang again.

"Hey, Dad. Happy Birthday."

"Thanks, Garrett. Guess it had to come sooner or later."

"How are you doing this morning? Do you want me to come over there or anything before the party, keep your company or something?"

"Thanks, son, I appreciate it, but I'm just going to get some breakfast, go see your mom, and run a few errands. I'll be back before this afternoon."

"Are you sure?"

"Yeah, it's no big deal. I'll see y'all at the party, right?"

"We'll be there, Dad."

"Ok, I'll see you then." I paused. "I love you, Garrett."

"I love you, too, Dad."

I turned off the TV, locked my front door, and drove off through the misty morning to the local pancake house where I was well known by the hostess and some of the waitresses.

"Can we get you your regular seat by the window this

morning?" The hostess asked me.

"That would be wonderful, thank you." I sat down in the booth where I had breakfast at least twice a week, and soon one of the waitresses approached me with a pot of coffee.

"Good morning, Mr. Winstead!" she said cheerfully. "The usual?"

"Yes ma'am, and good morning to you too, June," I responded brightly.

"Alrighty! Two pancakes, two fried eggs, two sausages, and coffee it is!" She poured out a cup for me and left the table.

During the course of my meal, a couple of other regulars who came in stopped at my table to speak to me, and one wished me a happy birthday. When I had finished, the waitress, June, asked me if there was anything else she could get for me this morning.

"You know, there is," I said. "Could I get two cups of coffee to go, with cream and no sugar, please?"

June smiled knowingly. "Yes sir. Two coffees to go, coming right up."

My next stop after breakfast was a quaint little flower shop, from where I emerged carrying a large bouquet of bright red carnations. Placing them carefully on the passenger seat, I got back in the car and drove for several miles, listening to the tires hum along the pavement. It was still early enough that not many people were out and about yet.

I drove out past the edge of the city and pulled off the road into a cemetery. As I parked the car, I suddenly realized I was visiting a graveyard in October and smiled to myself. My granddaughter would love the idea.

I carried the carnations on my arm and a coffee cup in each hand as I walked among the tombstones and monuments. The air was cool and still. I was alone with the dead. After walking for a few minutes, I came to the heart of the cemetery where my destination lay. When I reached the large, granite headstone, I stopped, knelt down, and placed the flowers in a bronze vase at the base of the stone.

"I know these were always your favorite," I said as I

lovingly arranged the scarlet flowers. Rising up, I placed one of the coffees on top of the stone above the chiseled name "Vicki Winstead." "There you are. Cream and no sugar, just the way you like it."

As I started drinking the other coffee, I looked at the tombstone. Only half of it was filled. The other half was vacant, smooth granite. I stood at the end of the grave for a good while as I drank my coffee, replaying memories from my marriage and wondering what to say.

"It's my birthday today," I said with a shrug. "The kids have a whole party planned out, but you know something? I would rather just stay here with you."

A tiny smile flitted across my face. "But I know that wouldn't be what you would want."

I don't know how long I stood there, but at last I looked up at the sky and knew I needed to be on my way.

Reluctantly I placed my hand on the headstone and caressed it gently. "Thank you for making me a better man," I said softly. "You and God made my life worth living. I'll see you soon, honey."

I drove and drove until I reached a point beyond the city called Rocky Butte, part of a volcanic cinder cone with a high bluff overlooking the city. It had been used in the old days as a lovers lane because of its striking view of the city lights at night. When I reached the top, I stood at the railing and stared out over Portland, reflecting on all the memories made there over the years. I thought of all the times Vicki and I had spent up here when we were dating, and as I observed the now-bustling city in the late morning light, I could remember all the places we had lived, worked, and raised our family. I began to whistle *Thanks for the Memories.*

There was a crunching of tires on gravel, and I looked back to see a patrol car parking behind mine. I walked over to see what was happening, and a tall policeman stepped out.

"Hey man, what do you think you're doing up here?" he demanded.

"Just looking at the city, officer," I said politely.

"Yeah, well, didn't you read the sign? This is government property. You aren't allowed to stop up here." He then jabbed his thumb at a sign that I must have overlooked which gave a two-hundred-dollar fine for parking in that area. My eyes widened.

"I'm sorry, I've been preoccupied. I didn't even notice the sign. I'll just move my car and be on my way."

He scoffed. "Uh, no, you're going to stand right here while I write you a ticket, and then you'll move your car. I need to see your ID, sir."

I shrugged and pulled out my wallet. I waited while he examined my license, now anxious to get back home. He looked up at me a couple of times to verify my picture, then remarked, "So it's your birthday today?"

"Yes, sir. I'm eighty-two today."

He studied me, then looked back at my license, turning it over in his hand. Then he shook his head and handed it back to me. "Have a nice day, Mr. Winstead."

I stuck my license back in my wallet. "You're not going to write me a ticket?"

He walked away from me and opened his patrol car door. "Happy birthday," he said with a smirk in his voice, and drove away.

When I got back to the house, I found my son Garrett, his wife Mary, and their son Darrin. Also, my daughter Lydia, and her husband, Matt, were there, along with my brother Dave, and his wife Susan. Several friends from church and work had already showed up and were helping decorate and set up for the big party in a few hours. I privately wished they wouldn't go to all the trouble, but I knew this was what they wanted to do. It was more for their benefit than mine, even if they didn't realize it themselves.

My daughter and daughter-in-law greeted me with kisses on the cheek and asked how I was feeling.

"I'm doing fine, I'm just a little tired. I've been all over the place this morning, so I think I'll just go upstairs and rest a little while before the party," I told them.

"That's a good idea," Lydia said. "That will give us time to get everything ready."

"Yes, so you go on up and don't worry about a thing. Everything is going to be lovely," Mary declared. I smiled at their kindness, and gave them each a hug before heading up to my room.

When I woke up later, I decided I would take a quick shower and dress for the evening ahead. I could already hear the commotion in the house and it was louder than before, now also coming from the backyard. I made my way downstairs and was greeted by more friends and family that had arrived during my nap. It seemed like the entire church congregation had come for the party. I saw Glenn and Brenda Hoffman, Carrie Stevenson with her husband, Tim, and their boys, and little Charlene with her father. It was almost impossible to get through the house because every single person stopped me to say happy birthday and give me a hug or handshake or kiss on the cheek (from the women). Like my retirement party, they all wanted to talk about old times. It saddened me to know that we didn't have enough time, much as I wanted to sit down with all of them and do just that.

But nobody said a word about what was to happen. Everyone who came was there for a time of fun, laughter, and wonderful fellowship. I knew my friends and family wanted this birthday to be my best. My son had set up the stereo system so my old musical favorites from the fifties and sixties floated out from the house and through the yard. Out on the back patio, the mouthwatering aroma of different foods filled the air. Besides a table full of cookies and pies, there were also shrimp and fine crab from the Pacific, crawfish from Louisiana, and barbecue from Texas with sides of corn, mashed potatoes, beans, and fried okra. In the middle of the all the desserts was a large cake that simply said: "Happy Birthday, Malachi! We love you!" There were two large number candles above the red lettering, a number eight and a number two. Garrett picked up a microphone and asked everyone to come out and sing Happy Birthday. They did, and I'm sure they were heard two blocks away. They followed up Happy Birthday with He's a Jolly Good Fellow, after which they all clamored for me to blow out the candles, and everyone clapped and cheered. Then Matt led us in a prayer for the food and we began the feast. I relished every dish, as they were all my favorite foods.

Before we cut the cake, my son asked me to say a few words. I was starting to feel that emotional pull again, but with their encouragement, I took the mic Garrett held out to me and stood up. A rare hush fell over the crowd.

"There are few men in the world as blessed as I am, to have so many wonderful people who care enough about me to be here tonight. I have been given more than I could ever deserve. I thank you all for coming. I love you all. I hope God blesses every single one of you here tonight as much as He has blessed me."

I couldn't go on for fear of tearing up, but my guests all stood up and clapped for almost a full minute as I handed the mic back to Garrett and walked over to get a slice of cake.

A few hours later, the party was over. The guests began to leave, coming to me with goodbyes on their lips and tears shining in their eyes. With each fond farewell and warm hug, I felt a tiny piece of me breaking away from my life in this world. This really was a final send-off, not only from my friends and family, but from myself as well.

I went and sat down beside what was left of the cake. Glancing over, I saw the two red number candles lying there and picked them up. I held up the "2" first, then the "8."

If I were twenty-eight again, I thought, and had to do it all over, I would do so much of it differently.

"Grandpa! Grandpa, there you are!"

My grandson, Darrin, swaggered over and held his hand up for a high-five. I gave it to him with a smile. "You have a good time tonight, kiddo?"

"Yes sir, it was fun. I ate a lot of your cake, Grandpa," he said proudly.

I chuckled. "Let's hope you don't get a stomachache, now. Your mother wouldn't like that."

"I never get stomachaches," he said importantly. "Oh,

Dad said to tell you that Mom and Aunt Lydia and Aunt Susan are about to leave now."

I quickly stood up. "We better go tell them goodbye, then, shouldn't we?"

Mary, Lydia, and my sister-in-law, Susan, stood in the entryway, holding bags of party supplies and food containers. But they put down everything they were holding when they saw me coming.

"There is no way I can thank you for everything you have done to make this...just the best birthday of my whole life," I told them from my heart. Susan immediately put her arms around me and said in my ear, "We love you, Malachi, and all you mean to us. It was a privilege to throw this party for you." She teared up and her voice broke. "We'll see you soon."

She abruptly broke off the hug, asking her husband, my brother Dave, to carry some things out to the car for her. Next, my daughter-in-law Mary hugged me tightly and kissed my cheek for the last time. "We'll miss you, Dad. I love you." Then she began to cry, and realizing she couldn't speak anymore, she picked up her purse and other bags. Garrett put his arm around her and held her close, guiding her out to the car. Lydia gave me a brief, firm hug and whispered a sweet goodbye before kissing my cheek and squeezing my hand. She didn't cry. She had always been less open about her emotions than Mary and my sister-in-law, but I knew she was feeling the pain of parting just as keenly as they were. Her husband Matt helped her carry the supplies out the front door.

Now it was only Darrin and I left in the entryway. After so many people having been in the house for several hours, it was strange to find it so quiet and empty. The clock on the wall showed ten-thirty.

"Guess it's just you and me, huh?" I said to Darrin. He stood leaning against the opposite wall, staring up at me. Suddenly he lunged across and flung his arms around me, hugging me with all his might.

"I'm gonna miss you more than anything, Grandpa," he blurted out. I wrapped my arms around him and held his little head against me, forcing back tears. Then the door opened, and Garrett and Dave came back in after seeing their wives off to their homes. I knew my brother and son were determined to stay with me to the end. My heart went out to them.

"I need to go up to my room to rest and pray," I told them as they gathered around me. "It won't be long now, and I want to spend some time with the Lord."

"Do you want us to come and be with you? So you aren't alone?" Dave asked, putting a hand on my shoulder. I read the same question in Garrett's eyes, but I shook my head.

"I won't be alone. I'm never alone," I said with a smile. "It's been a long evening, and I'm worn out, but I'll be fine."

"Can we get you anything, Dad?" Garrett asked in concern.

"No, son. Just knowing you are here in this house with me is all I need."

"Me too, Grandpa?" Darrin asked hopefully.

"Especially you," I told him in a low voice. "I'll see you in a little while," I added for them all to hear as I started up the steps to my room to rest for the second time that day. Closing the door, it occurred to me that maybe I should review all of the messages I said I would try to deliver before I began saying my prayers.

"Enter by the narrow gate; for wide is the gate and broad is the way that leads to destruction, and there are many who go in by it. Because narrow is the gate and difficult is the way which leads to life, and there are few who find it. -Matthew 7:13-14

Chapter 12

The ACA

Garrett and Dave walked into the living room. Darrin had already turned on the TV and was watching the news.

"Turn that off," Garrett told his son.

"Aww, but Dad, it's just the news!" he protested.

"You heard me," his father repeated, and Darrin unwillingly punched the power button, letting the remote drop onto the couch beside him.

Garrett walked over to the window and leaned against the wall, keeping his eyes fixed on the empty street outside. Dave sat down next to Darrin on the couch and stretched his arm out along the back behind Darrin's head. Darrin looked around at them, puzzled by their strange and tense behavior.

"So what's going on? What are we doing here, Dad?" he demanded. "I thought you said Grandpa was going away. Does he need us to go with him?"

Garrett pushed himself away from the wall with his elbow and sat down in Malachi's armchair. He hesitated for a moment, and then said slowly, "I think you're old enough to understand now, Darrin."

"Understand what?" Darrin looked expectantly at him. Garrett tilted his head from side to side, popping his neck before nodding toward Dave. "Maybe you better hear this from your uncle. He can tell you all about it."

Dave flicked Darrin's shoulder.

"Listen here, boy," he said quietly, "I'll give you some information that they'll never tell you in school."

Wide-eyed, Darrin shifted on the couch to face his great-uncle, all ears. Garrett sat across from them with his elbows propped on the chair arms, his fingers laced together and a clouded look in his eyes. He was looking out the window again.

"It all started several years ago," Dave began, "Right around the time you were born. It was a good idea at first. Free health care for every American, and they called it the 'Affordable Care Act'." Dave scoffed. "What a joke that turned out to be. Within three years, it became a financial nightmare. Well, the government got desperate and did all it could to spike taxes as high as possible to pay for this black hole it had created that was sucking the economic life out of the country."

"What happened?" Darrin asked breathlessly.

"First of all, the rich simply moved out of America because they were getting hit the hardest with the tax increase, but that just made everything worse. By that time over seventy-five percent of Americans were getting free health care. But because taxes were so high, people wanted more and better care for their tax dollars. Of all these, half of them never paid any taxes at all. Then we had all the illegal aliens storming across the borders to get free medical care, too. There were demands that the 'Affordable Care Act' should include other things like cosmetic surgery. It was as if everyone was just obsessed with every kind of medical care that was available, wanting to milk the system dry with their demands."

Garrett looked away from his window-watching vigil to glance at the clock. He picked up a pen from the small table beside him and began flipping it end over end on his knee.

"Don't stop there," he said to Dave as he leaned back and pressed the backs of his fists against his eyes. His voice had grown hard. "Tell him everything."

"The so-called 'affordable' act had become such a financial burden that America was literally on the edge of going broke," Dave said to Darrin. "Something had to be done, and fast. So, there was a closed-door meeting with the president and his cabinet, the House, and the Senate. An emergency meeting. No press allowed. That group met off and on for three days while the country waited to see whether she would rise or fall. Finally, those in the meeting voted in some amendments to the wretched 'Affordable Care Act' law to fix the problems that had become so dire."

Dave was growing more and more agitated the more he went on, and suddenly got up from his seat and went to the window. As he walked he added, "Oh, by the way, Darrin, all elected officials, past, present, future, or even retired, would be exempt from these new amendments. Ha!" Dave gritted his teeth. "What a bunch of cowards they were."

Darrin got up and followed his great-uncle to the window, eager to hear more. Dave didn't look at him, but instead out into the dark, empty street.

"It just makes my blood boil thinking about it. Garrett," he said without turning around, "Tell your son exactly what they did when they passed those amendments."

Garrett rubbed his left temple and crossed his arms. "The new, revised law stated that anyone found to have a terminal illness would be given an opportunity to end their life. But, if they could not or would not, then the government gave authority to the ACA to establish a department called..." He inhaled sharply. "'The Human Assistance Division'."

Dave made a fist and pressed it hard against the windowpane. Darrin was staring at his father.

"What's that?" he asked.

"The Human Assistance Division's job was to seek out, find, and terminate any and every person with a terminal illness. Of course, this was going to save money. Then they started looking at anyone on death row or just prisoners in general with no possibility of parole. Why not throw them into the mix too? They weren't valued members of society, they were a waste of skin in the government's eyes. But soon, those kinds of people weren't enough. Their deaths weren't enough to pay for the nightmare the government forced on us. After awhile they quietly began going after the mentally ill under the guise that it was for the well-being of the country, and this was the humane thing to do. The government said their end would be painless and..." Garrett practically spat out the next word, "merciful."

"End?" Dave spoke up from the window. "End? They were just killing them off, like Hitler and the Jews. What a society we have become, preying on the weak, sick, and mentally disturbed to save a few dollars for a tummy-tuck while convincing people this is all being done for their own good."

Garrett stood up. "Dave, it's twelve o'clock. I'm going to check on Dad and see if he needs anything or wants to come down here with us and then I'll make some coffee."

Malachi's son walked out of the room on his mission.

"Who were Hitler and the Jews?" Darrin asked his uncle.

Dave leaned his back against the window, folding his arms. "You never heard of Hitler and his Nazi party? I can't believe what they don't teach you in school these days. Hitler was practically the inspiration for the law we have in place now."

"What are you talking about?"

Dave leaned in and said very quietly, "Death squads, son. To get rid of everybody who was deemed unhealthy for the sake of the healthy."

"Death squads?" Darrin's eyes were huge. "We have those in America?"

"Well of course, they aren't just running around in the open. But they have very stealthily started to go after alcoholics and drug addicts, now. If you're a drug addict and have been through a drug rehab clinic three times, they determine you to be a financial and medical burden to society, as well as incurable. So the ACA takes them to a place they call 'drug camps'. They're usually out in the middle of nowhere so they can't wander off. Then they're given access to all the drugs they want, and as much of them as they want. Guess what happens?"

"What?" Darrin breathed.

"Their loved ones get a report a short while later that their family member who was taken away simply died of a drug overdose."

"But, but they can't do that!" Darrin spluttered, his mouth hanging open. "Can they?"

"It's what our government does best," Dave said moodily.

"Oh, and here's another fun fact for you. The ACA also requires all drug stores to sell a painless suicide kit. It's one of their nice ways to save on some of the death squads."

Garrett re-entered the living room. "Dad is still praying. He said he's fine and he's going to stay up there until he's needed. Coffee's going," he added quietly, and resumed his seat.

"How would the government know who is really sick or not, Uncle Dave?" Darrin asked.

"Let me tell you how this cute little thing works. The government will fine any hospital or doctor who doesn't report a person with a terminal illness. But that's not even the best part. There are lots of doctors working in secret to treat terminally ill patients, and when they've gotten all their money they simply turn those patients over to the government to collect reward. These doctors are the scum of the earth."

"The doctors are bad guys?" Darrin gasped. He turned to his father. "And you and Mom made me get a booster shot this year!" he said accusingly.

"Thanks, Uncle Dave," Garrett said wearily.

Dave put his arm around Darrin.

"Not all of them are evil, kiddo."

"Does Grandpa have a terminal illness?" Darrin said in a low voice, as if it were a great secret.

Dave looked down at his great-nephew, mussed his hair, started to answer, then saw the clock.

"Hey, boys, it's twelve-o-two. I'm going out on the front porch and sit awhile." He headed into the entryway where they heard the creak of the screen door. "Why don't you tell your son what's wrong with his grandfather," he called back to Garrett before the door slammed shut.

Garrett looked at his son, who was still standing where his uncle had left him by the window. Garrett gestured toward him, and the two of them sat down on the couch.

"Dad, does Grandpa have a terminal illness?" the boy asked, his mouth turned down at the corners.

His father shook his head. "To help track down every

person who is sick, the government passed a law that demands that every person, on their sixty-fifth birthday, must report to an assigned hospital for a physical. If you pass the physical with a clean bill of health, you're free to go. But if you are deemed to have a terminal illness, you don't get to go home."

"You never leave the hospital?"

"No. But then again, when you turn seventy-five, you are once again required to visit your assigned hospital for another physical. And you go through the same process."

"But Dad, I still don't get it. If Grandpa isn't sick, what's going on with him now? Why is he leaving? Why are we all saying goodbye?" Darrin's eyes squinted in confusion.

Garrett pressed his lips together. "Darrin, your grandfather is in very good health. What's wrong with him is his age."

"His age? He's eighty-two," Darrin said, puzzled. "That isn't bad, is it?"

"Unfortunately, for him it is. In the last amendment of the ACA that the government secretly passed, it says thirty days before your eighty-second birthday, you must report to the hospital for one more physical. But this time around, if your health is still good, you will be allowed to leave for only thirty days. On their birthday, all US citizens eighty-two years of age are required by law to return to their hospital for their 'humane and painless' death."

Darrin's mouth hung open. His chest rose and fell with rapid breathing. "But why? Why are they doing this, Dad?"

Garrett rubbed his forehead. His voice was bitter. "Darrin, the government decided that everyone who reaches the age of eighty-two will in the next few years likely have some type of serious, long-term illness or other issue that will cause the ACA to become more overburdened and unstable than it already is. That's why they chose this method of eliminating the problem early, in their way of thinking."

"But that's so wrong!" Darrin exploded, his face twisted in righteous indignation.

"You're right. It's very wrong, Darrin. But it is the law,

whether we like it or not."

Darrin sat staring at the black TV screen, his mind going a hundred miles an hour.

"But Grandpa didn't go back to the hospital today."

"That's right. And do you understand why?"

Darrin looked at his father if he thought maybe he knew, but he was not quite sure. Garrett put his arm around him.

"Your grandfather is a Christian, Darrin, and he's a faithful one, too. He can't be a party to taking his own life or freely giving it away like the law demands. Our lives are in God's hands, not our own. So he signed a form the last time he was at the hospital a month ago, stating he would not volunteer to return himself to be put to death."

"But Dad, if Grandpa told them he wasn't coming back, why are we here? Are we going to help him run away?"

"You can ask your Uncle Dave again on that one. This was his idea." Garrett stood up and stretched. "I'll go check on your Grandpa again."

Darrin walked out onto the front porch. The silver moon was a crescent in the sky. Dave was sitting in a straight-back chair, leaning it back against the wall so it rested on two legs while he looked at his phone screen. Darrin joined him, hopping up to sit on the porch railing.

"Uncle Dave?"

"Mm-hmm?"

"Dad says I should ask you what we're doing here tonight."

He kept looking at his phone, and Darrin cocked his head, waiting. Suddenly Dave's chair thumped forward, landing loudly on all four legs, startling the boy. Dave's face was very stern.

"I'll tell you why we're here and exactly what we're going to do. Very soon, there's gonna be some black vehicles driving up this street heading for this house. A bunch of guys dressed in black will pile out, and they'll have weapons. But you see this box?"

Dave gestured toward the crate nestled in the darkest corner of the porch. Darrin, his mouth agape, nodded.

"I have three AK-47s in there. Clip-loaded. Your dad and I

will take out those guys from right here on this porch before they can get all the way across the yard. You will be hiding behind the hedge there at the edge of the yard. When the shooting starts, you'll jump out and take out the drivers and anyone else standing nearby."

"Really?" Darrin's eyes grew wider and wider. "But I've never shot an AK before."

"You can handle it. Then you'll stay here and guard the house while your dad and I load the bodies into the cars and drive them down into the river where they won't be found for a long, long time."

Darrin sat frozen on the porch railing with one hand wrapped around one of the posts attached to the eave, his mouth hanging open. As he pondered what was about to happen, he could feel his blood racing faster.

At that moment, his dad opened the door.

"Darrin, you need to come into the house now."

"But what about Uncle Dave's plan?"

Darrin looked back at Dave, expecting him to tell Garrett what he had just told him. But Dave was already leaning his chair back on two legs again against the wall. He winked at Darrin.

"Kiddo, we wouldn't really do that."

"Thanks a lot for winding him up, Uncle Dave," Garrett said, putting his hand on Darrin's shoulder to steer him inside. Darrin realized he had just been had by his great-uncle.

"Yeah, maybe it's better if you take him in before he shoots somebody," Dave commented. Darrin made a face at him.

"Ok, so I still don't know why we're here," he said to his father as he closed the door behind them.

"Well since your great-uncle was obviously of no help there, I'll tell you. This Eighty-Two law has been in effect for about five years now, and there are a lot of stories about what happens when the HAD comes after someone. Some very bad things have happened to ACA agents who come to pick up their targets, but even worse things have happened to those who resist extraction or retaliate against the HAD. We are here to be witnesses that nothing happens. If the HAD knows people are watching them, they will be more careful to follow the law and not hurt your grandfather when they take him. We're also here to see that they don't damage anything else, either."

"Wait...so the Human Assistance Division is coming here tonight to take Grandpa away?"

"Yes. Because he didn't sign his life away, they have to bring him in," said Garrett sadly.

"But Grandpa couldn't hurt anyone!" Darrin exclaimed. "Why would they–"

"Let me just say this." Garrett bent down on eye level with his son, putting his hands on his shoulders. "If we were not here, and your grandpa didn't want to be taken, I don't think they would be able to."

Darrin stared at his father. "Really?"

"Trust me, son. There is a lot about your grandfather that he wouldn't want you to know."

Darrin wasn't sure what to make of that. "So, why am I here, me, specifically?"

Garrett sighed. "Because you are growing up, Darrin. And it's high time you understood the kind of world we're living in. It's affecting you more than you realize, with all these laws that have been passed in the time since you were born. I hate to say this to you, but you're going to grow up in a cruel, hard world. I wish I could make it easier for you, but I can't."

"But how come I never heard about the Eighty-Two law in school or on the news?"

"Because nearly everybody is ashamed of what is being done, and no one will talk about it. The government keeps it quiet. And when somebody turns eighty, nobody wants to talk to them about what's going to happen to them later. Nobody wants to think about or be reminded of what will happen two years down the road."

"Well, somebody needs to talk about it!" Darrin exclaimed. His face grew thoughtful. "Maybe I'll talk about it sometime," he said quietly to himself.

They heard a quick sound from the front porch of chair legs scraping the porch floor. Garrett straightened up, his eyes wary.

"Darrin, somebody is out there," he said in a low, urgent voice. "Listen to me. When they come in, don't say anything. We don't want to jeopardize the situation. These men are trained assassins and they have a court order from a judge to take your grandfather."

Garrett looked directly into his son's eyes again. "Do you understand, Darrin Winstead? We are only here as witnesses. We cannot interfere. Remember! Do not say anything. Anything! These men can take you to jail or worse."

"I won't say anything, Dad," Darrin promised, beginning to cry.

Garrett bit his lip hard. He pressed his son's head against his chest and blinked fiercely.

Outside, the sound of car doors opening and closing along with approaching footsteps cracked through the stillness of the night.

For to me, to live is Christ, and to die is gain.
-Philippians 1:21

Chapter 13

Last Stop for the Night

Dave rose from his chair and stuffed his phone into his back pocket, moving to stand in front of the door as the men in black walked across the front lawn. Two of them broke away from the group to go around back, one on each side, while the other three strode up to the front porch. The man in the lead, wearing a black officer's uniform, leveled his gun directly at Dave.

"Look, guys–"

His words were cut off as the leader shoved him away from the door and up against the wall, holding him there with his gun barrel pressed tightly against Dave's chest.

"Get your hands up and keep them up!" he ordered while a second man searched Dave for weapons. "Who are you?"

"I'm David Winstead, brother of Malachi Winstead who lives here," Dave answered quickly, keeping his hands raised.

The officer stepped back to give Dave enough breathing room, but kept his gun on him. "Where's your identification?"

Dave handed it to him as the officer demanded, "What are you doing here?"

"Making sure there's no trouble here tonight for anyone." Dave emphasized on the last word. The third man scanned his tablet.

"Malachi Winstead does have a brother named David Winstead, sir," he said. "His ID checks out."

The officer didn't take his eyes or his weapon off Dave. "No health warrants?"

"No, sir."

The officer lowered his gun ever so slightly. At the same time, Dave let his hands go down toward his sides. Suddenly, the officer lunged forward, pressing his forearm across Dave's throat and pinning him against the wall of the house again. "Who is in the house? Tell me now!"

Dave gagged as he tried to get his words out. "My... brother...his son...and grandson."

The officer leaned forward so their faces were almost touching.

"And what are they doing in there?" he growled.

"Just...want...to make...sure…everything goes...ok..." Dave choked.

The officer held him a moment longer, then released him. Dave bent over, rubbing his neck and coughing. He looked up to see the officer still holding a gun on him. Dave wanted nothing more in that moment than to snatch that gun out of the officer's hands and turn his own weapon on him. But Dave also knew he would never live to make the move.

"Why didn't your brother come to the hospital today?"

"Because he's a Christian, and can't be a party to his own death," Dave answered stridently.

When he said that, Dave felt the tension dissipate somewhat as the officers and his men looked at each other.

"He's a Christian," the officer mused. "Alright. Let's just go in there and get him." He stepped forward, pushing Dave out of the way. Another man trained his gun on Dave now while the officer examined the door, pressing his hand against the screen. He turned on Dave.

"Is there a bomb on the other side of this door?"

"A bomb?" Dave's mouth was dry. "No, sir! I promise you. No bomb."

The officer stepped closer to him. "You better not be lying to us," he said in a dangerous voice.

"I'm telling you the truth. No one's going to try and stop you," Dave pleaded. "Here, I could open–"

"Halt!" the officer roared, and now Dave had three guns

pointed at him. Raising his hands in compliance and none-too-well-disguised anger, he fell back a step. But the officer grabbed him by the front of his shirt and shoved him over in front of the door.

"Open it. You're going in first."

As the four men entered the house, Garrett and Darrin moved to stand in the doorway between the living room and the entryway. The officer stopped when he saw them, telling them to raise their hands. Darrin stared down the gun barrel pointed at him, and Garrett managed to shift his body so he was standing in front of his son.

The agent with the tablet gave them a quick search and said, "They're clean."

"Who are you two?" the officer said coldly.

"I'm Garrett Winstead," said Garrett in a level voice. "This is my son, Darrin Winstead."

"Come on, give me your ID," said the agent with the tablet, snapping his fingers impatiently.

They handed over their IDs as the officer in charge looked around.

"What are you doing here?" he demanded. Dave rolled his eyes.

"Malachi Winstead is my father, and we are here to be witnesses that all goes well with his extraction," Garrett said firmly.

"Go well?" the officer snapped. "I'll make that call. And I'm warning all of you, if you make one bit of trouble, I'll be the one to finish it. Now, where is the old man?"

Garrett took a tentative step forward. "He's upstairs in the bedroom."

"Is he alive?"

"Yes, sir."

The officer in charge turned to his men.

"Stay here and keep an eye on these two." He jerked his head toward where Garrett and Darrin were now standing huddled just inside the living room. He waved his gun at Dave. "You're going to show me where your brother is."

****

I heard them coming.

I sat at my desk in my room, my old Bible open in front of me. Any minute now, they would come bursting through the door. I heard a man shout briefly outside and some banging noises, then a short silence before I heard the screen door open, then the front door. I closed my eyes, praying my family members weren't hurt.

They were in the house.

I looked back down at the passage I was reading.

But He laid his right hand on me, saying, "Fear not, I am the first and the last, and the living one. I died, and behold I am alive forevermore, and I have the keys of Death and Hades.

"Father, give me strength," I said aloud just before my bedroom door was thrust open.

A man dressed in a black officer's uniform carrying a gun pushed my brother in before him. I stood up, keeping one hand on the Bible beside me.

The officer, who I had no doubt of being a HAD agent, prowled toward me like a lion stalking its prey. "Well, old man. You didn't show up for your doctor's appointment. Which means we're going to have to do this the hard way."

A few minutes later the officer was marching Dave and me back down the stairs, me with zip ties securing my wrists behind my back. My legs were also banded together, but with enough space allowing me to take short steps. As we rejoined the others, I saw my son and grandson. My arms flexed automatically, wanting to embrace them one last time.

"Officer, could I say goodbye to my family?"

"Sorry, old man." He checked his watch. "You should have done that already. I don't have time for this, and we have to go."

I felt the cold tip of his gun barrel against my back as he pushed me toward the door. I looked back at my family for as long as I could before the officer forced me to keep walking across the porch and down the steps toward the black SUVs waiting in the street. The other agents filed slowly out of the house behind us, keeping their weapons on my family until they all reconvened on the lawn with two more who came from around the side of the house, and moved in formation back to the vehicles. I managed to twist around one last time and saw Dave, Garrett, and Darrin all standing on the porch. Darrin was crying.

A big black truck sped up from just out of sight beyond the reach of the street lamp glow. As I was held on the curb, it pulled up in front of me and one of the agents opened the back of it. When the light came on, I saw a man and a woman inside with their hands and feet bound, and tape was stretched across their mouths. The woman looked to have put up some resistance, for her face was bruised and bloody. I looked at the man and saw his eyes were wide with terror as he pulled on his restraints.

But they weren't the only people in the van. On the floor, under the feet of the two sitting up, were two filled body bags.

"Busy night," the officer commented. One of the other agents grabbed a roll of tape from the front seat and started to tear off a piece. I turned and looked at the officer in charge. He was drawing off his black gloves one finger at a time, but when he felt me staring at him, he looked up and we locked eyes.

"Wait," he said, holding out one hand. He jerked his glove off the rest of the way and stepped very close to me.

"This won't be necessary," he said in a low voice, nodding his head toward the tape. "Will it?"

"No, sir," I answered. He smirked and ordered the other man to hold off.

"Alright, load him up and let's go."

Two agents gripped me by the elbows and hoisted me up into the back of the van with the man and woman. Before they closed the door, I heard my brother calling out to the officer.

"Hey! Nothing will happen to my brother on the way, right?"

"Listen to them, trying to find any way of comforting themselves," I heard the officer mutter to one of his colleagues.

He raised his voice to answer Dave. "No. We're going straight to the hospital from here. This is our last stop for the night."

He had started walking back to one of the cars when I heard him stop and add in a professionally detached manner, "If your brother is a Christian, Mr. Winstead, he'll be fine."

Fine. I'll be fine.

"Oh, and if you want the body, you better have your undertaker there before three or it goes to the incinerator," the officer finished. I heard one of the car doors slam as he got in, and then the door to our vehicle was closed, and I was encased in total darkness.

As we jolted forward with the movement of the truck while it drove away, I sat thinking again back over the past month and all the people I had met. All the stories I had heard. All the messages I had been given. And suddenly, I was strangely glad. Finally, it would be over. Finally, I could go home to the Lord, and be with my Vicki forever. One day, the rest of my family would meet us there.

And if God allowed it, I would deliver the messages to those souls in heaven, while their loved ones back on earth dreamed of the day they would see them again.

THE END

Chapter 13

Yea, though I walk through the valley of the shadow of death, I will fear no evil; For You are with me; Your rod and Your staff, they comfort me. -Psalm 23:4

Other books from this author

A compelling novel about an election year in America, lifted straight out of today's evening news.

The Speaker **weaves a mystery throughout the mayhem of America's political arena, going straight to the heart of what it truly means to be an American.**

The country is in legislative, economical, and moral turmoil. The next presidential election looms near, and political parties are at each other's throats. The nation's future rests on uneasy ground. But amidst all the chaos going into November's preparations, one voice will stand out from the crowd. A voice speaking not only of freedom for the nation, but freedom for the soul. Nobody knows who he is or where he came from, but soon every American will know his name.

Available as an e-Book from:

This 399-page soft-cover book is available from wvbs.org

This wonderful novel will hold your attention to the very last page.

Reader's Favorite gives *The House* a five-star review.

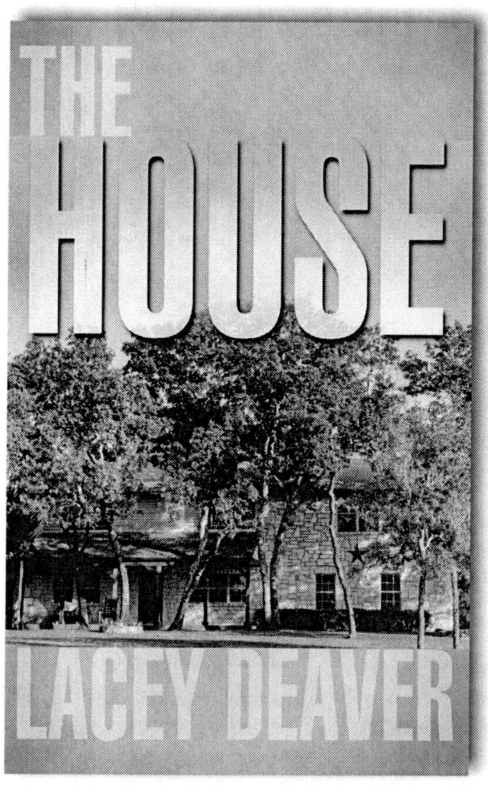

The House by Lacey Deaver is a good Christian story from beginning to end. Cheri is a troubled young woman running for her life. She hides in a truck in Seattle and, after three days without food and water, she escapes from the truck in a small Texas town. Cheri has no money and no place to go, so as she wanders the town she is picked up by the local Sheriff who brings her to the "house" of Margret and Carl Hanna. Daniel is a long time friend of the Hannas and often stays in the guesthouse. Cheri is mean and angry at the recent development in her life. Margret and Daniel befriend her over time and slowly she changes. The strength of growing friendships and belief in God is the crux of this heartwarming story.

The House will make you smile and make you cry, but mostly it will keep you glued to the book until you reach the end. It is a very fast paced story and only took a few hours of reading to finish, but I was really sorry to come to the final page and leave my new friends behind. Lacey Deaver is a marvelous storyteller. She has spiced the book with just enough suspense, drama, romance and uncertainty to keep me reading with great anticipation of the ending. I absolutely adored each of the characters and the plot is flawless. This book is perfect.

-*Reader's Favorite* review **www.ReadersFavorite.com**

Also available in E-book form

Reader's Favorite gives *Good & Evil* a five-star review.

Good & Evil by Lacey Deaver is an excellent book. Jack Krantz is the 'disbelieving in God,' mean man. Tyler Emerson strongly believes in God and always does the right thing. Jack is a very rich man and wants to become richer, even if it means destroying other people. Tyler is wheelchair bound and without means of income and believes God will provide for all of his needs. Jack has taken Tyler's wife, destroyed their business partnership and is now trying to evict him and his sister Elizabeth from their home. When Jack has an accident that comes very close to killing him, it is Tyler who visits him every day in the hospital, trying to convince him to accept Jesus or risk going to Hell. Though no one can see or hear the two spirits following Jack on his path of recovery, the reader hears the debate of who shall claim him upon his death. Each argument is backed with a biblical truth and each paragraph ends in a passage from a book in the bible. The ending was one I did not at all see coming, but was a perfect finish.

Good & Evil was very different in a very good way. I was totally caught up by both sides – liking one and being disappointed for the other. The story could have been a standalone but the bible quotes made it so much more realistic. I found myself wanting to help Tyler and witness to Jack because Lacey Deaver made it seem so real. Whether or not you believe in God, this is a great book, pitting good against evil in man and how it can play out. Do not pass up Good & Evil; it is an inspiration.

-*Reader's Favorite* review **www.ReadersFavorite.com**

Also available in E-book form

Books from WVBS

–Searching for Truth Study Guides–

These study guides, written by **John Moore**, area great resource as a companion to the *Searching for Truth* DVD, or used on their own as a workbook. The material is suitable for individual study or used in any Bible class setting. The text follows the same chapter structure and is nearly a word-for-word transcript of the DVD.

The study guides include extended question sections, including a "Section Review" after each section and a "Chapter Review" at the end of each chapter. To close-out the chapter there is a "Digging Deeper" section, which includes additional verses on the subject matter that are not used in the text. The answer to every question can be found in the Answer Key section at the end of the book. Additionally, six teaching charts are included in the book. These 8.5 x 11 inch, full-color charts cover popular issues such as, "The Book of Daniel & God's Kingdom," "Where do we go when we die?," "Modern Churches Timeline," "The Ten Commandments?," Baptism's significance, and the Church as God's spiritual house.

English Study Guide

Spanish Study Guide

Over 120,000 printed!

Russian

Korean

Swahili

Also available in E-book form

Reader's Favorite gives *Transformed: A Spiritual Journey* a four-star review.

Transformed: A Spiritual Journey by Lance Mosher is a profound and inspirational book that documents the important events of the author's life. This spiritual autobiography is peppered with events in life, topics of conversation, and dialogues that speak about the author's emotional and intellectual struggles. The book shows the providence of God and will help readers with open minds to wrestle with themselves and the Lord. The book has spiritual answers to many questions that are already in the minds of readers, and will convince readers about the truths that exist in their beliefs. The book teaches readers to love and respect God, pray regularly, and lead a clean and good life.

The book is uplifting and helpful to all those who want to contemplate the teachings in their lives and the entire essence of their existence. The author's simple and succinct style makes it easy for readers to connect with what he is trying to convey. The author pulls readers into his world and many of his experiences are relatable. The book helps transform many readers, where the truth will set them free instead of debates, opinions or speculations.

God's presence is again reiterated through the author's words and he does an excellent job by helping readers understand Jesus Christ. This thought provoking book is definitely a good guide for all those readers who are trying to understand the Bible and the Lord in a better way.

-*Readers' Favorite* review **www.ReadersFavorite.com**

Also available in E-book form

Reader's Favorite gives *The Truth About Moral Issues* a four-star review.

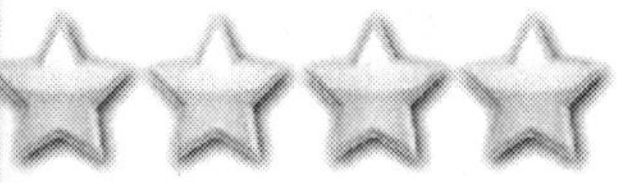

The Truth About Moral Issues by Don Blackwell is a book dedicated to help share advice and insight on the moral issues that face people - young and old - in this day and age. While mainly focusing on issues that youths tend to be faced with, this book reads well for anyone. Beginning with Tattoos and Piercings and ending up with what one must do to be saved, Don Blackwell goes through the figurative ABC's of behavior and getting back into God's good graces.

This book is a decidedly Christian themed book, and is an accurate representation of traditionalist Christian values. Christian parents no doubt will consider The Truth About Moral Issues to be a must-read for every one of their preteens and teenagers. While told in a dry tone of rhetoric, the passages themselves contain a sardonic wit that will not necessarily leave you laughing out loud, but will certainly have you raise an amused eyebrow.

I really liked some of the chapter art. It was clear that the artists were moving in a creative direction with the pieces and I really enjoyed that I wasn't sure if it was digitally rendered or drawn using colored pencils -that's the mark of a good artist right there! As a young preacher himself, Don is a pretty trusted authority in the area of morals within a Christian context, so it's wise to take his thoughts and opinions to heart. He backs up his ideas with quotes and analysis from the Bible, which helps to clarify things most excellently!

-*Reader's Favorite* review **www.ReadersFavorite.com**

Also available in E-book form

Reader's Favorite gives *Men in the Making* a four-star review.

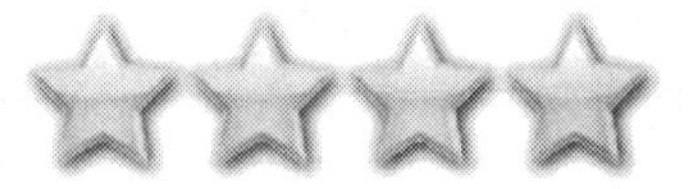

In Men in the Making, authors Kyle Butt, Stan Butt Jr., and JD Schwartz talk to young teenage boys about what it means to grow from adolescence into manhood based on God's biblical standards. They candidly and creatively address such topics as how to choose proper role models, why a godly man should defend the weak, ways to show honor to elders and other adults, how to get along with your parents, winning the battle against sexual temptation and, most importantly, how to choose the right woman to marry and spend the rest of your life with - all this from a Christian perspective. The added bonus to the book was that the authors listed links at the end of each chapter that take you to other sites where you can receive instruction on various moral dilemmas, also all from a Christian perspective. This addition alone makes the book a valuable resource long after the last page is turned.

I read Kyle Butt, Stan Butt Jr., and JD Schwartz's book from the perspective of a Christian parent who is also well versed in the scriptures. I read it with a critical eye, checking to see whether the authors' doctrine was sound. The question in my mind during the entire time was: would I allow my teenager to receive these three men's biblical instruction? The answer is a resounding yes. Kyle Butt, Stan Butt Jr., and JD Schwartz's conversational tone came across to me as a couple of big brothers sitting around the campfire with some young men and 'keeping it real' about girls, life, and God. I would definitely recommend this book to my teenager and to parents and youth leaders looking for ways to approach these delicate subjects with their teenage boys.

-*Reader's Favorite* review **www.ReadersFavorite.com**

Also available in E-book form

Reader's Favorite gives *Songs of Deliverance* a five-star review.

Bible study is an important practice for anyone trying to develop and maintain a positive Christian attitude. With many different approaches for understanding the word of God, Songs of Deliverance by Debra Griffin Mitchell offers a fresh, straight-forward guide for identifying examples of deliverance. Debra Griffin Mitchell defines deliverance as 'rescue from danger, defeat or suffering; release from bondage; relief or freedom from dread or fear'. She also asserts that we all need it and provides definite biblical evidence of God's care for His people. Clearly comparing what biblical personages were delivered from and delivered to, Songs of Deliverance demonstrates the power of prayer, faith and repentance. Even when the final result of prayer is death, the soul is better off when it belongs to one of God's faithful. A sure place in heaven is a small price to pay for continuing to praise God and live by Christ's example in the face of the evil and distractions in today's world.

Arranged in thirteen insightful, easy to follow and inspirational chapters, Songs of Deliverance begins with songs and prayers from the Old Testament, moving up through the New Testament and even those used by the early Church. Each chapter is clearly designed for a class or individuals to follow to appreciate the depth and complexity of the stories and events presented in Scripture. Topics to think about and discuss are spread throughout the presentation of the songs and an application of the lesson to everyday life concludes each chapter. This text is well researched and extensive footnotes and the citation of sources are included. Debra Griffin Mitchell has taken key sections of the Bible and made them easily accessible to students of any age.

-*Reader's Favorite* review **www.ReadersFavorite.com**

Also available in E-book form

CPSIA information can be obtained
at www.ICGtesting.com
Printed in the USA
FFOW03n1940010917
39463FF